Mountain Yarns and Prairie Tales

From the Pen of Big Irv Lampman

Mountain Yarns and Prairie Tales by Irv Lampman

Published by PREMIUM PRESS AMERICA

Copyright © 2003 Irv Lampman

All rights reserved. No part of this book may be reproduced or transmitted in any form or by any means, electronic or mechanical, including photocopying, recording, or by any information storage and retrieval system, without prior written permission of the Publisher, except where permitted by law.

ISBN 978-0-9637733-7-1

Library of Congress Catalog Card Number: 2003103714

PREMIUM PRESS AMERICA gift books are available at special discounts for premiums, sales promotions, fundraising, or educational use. For details contact the Publisher at P.O. Box 58995, Nashville TN 37205-8995, or phone toll-free 800/891-7323 or 615/353-7902, or fax 615/353-7905.

For more information visit our website at www.premiumpressamerica.com

Design by Armour&Armour

First Edition May 2003
  5 6 7 8 9 10

DEDICATION

First, let me say, this book is dedicated to Mom and Dad Lampman, who believed in me when no one else did.

To Sandy, my little lady, who believes in me, shares my life, and brightens my days with her smile.

To Lilian Beach, whom I class as one of the inspirations for these tales. She lived life like a steam train and is a great teller of stories.

To Helen and Jim Vest, our best friends.

Special thank you to Danny Vanhouten and to Sue Ann Kumlien for all their support over the years.

To Dave Friske, who'll ride the river even when the boat's leakin'.

And to Winston Whitford—thanks for a lifetime of friendship.

CONTENTS

Cowboys and Miners

Ghost Town	2
When Death Came A-ridin' A Horseback	4
The Men with the Tied-down Guns	6
Born A Hundred Years Too Late	9
Why	10
The Last of the Breed	12
Starfire: We Won't See His Like Again	13
Confrontation	14
The Devil Horse	16
Ten Thousand on the Prod	19
Old Higgins	22
The Mysterious Killer of Caufield County	24
A Visitor in Camp	30
Cookee	32
The Sobbin' Killer of the Kalahari	34
The Banquet	39
The Legend of Finnegan's Well	42
A Tale at Fifty Below	45
Greed	48
The Horror at Old Dry Wells	52

Ghost Stories

The Legend of Wilson's Slough	56
The House on Haunted Hill	58
The Nature of the Beast	60
Imaginations	61
A Bad Night on Scarecrow Hill	62
The Coach	64
Still Mr. President	66
The Face on the Stone	68
The Bell Witch	71
Nighttime on the Moors	72
The Mystery of O'Flaverty's Keep	74
Night Hauntings and Reflections	76
Battleground	79
The Gargoyle	80
Cassie	82
The Anniversary	84
Vanishing Oliver Larch	86
The Light on Chapel Hill	87
The Rider of Phantom Hill	89
Pumpkin Hollow	91

Stories of the Sea
The Devil Fish	94
The Mystery of the *Mary Celeste*	97
Something Drawing Near	98
The Maelstrom	100
The Voice	102
Skeleton Island	106
The Dutchman	109
Hell Ship	111
The Sargasso	116

Railroad Stories and Truckers
When the Reaper Comes	120
The Story of the Strangest Love	122
Wreck of the Twelve 51	124
The Whistle in the Night	126
The Surprise	128
The Road Is My Home	130

Sentimental Poems and Stories
Halloween: What I Wouldn't Give To Be a Kid Again	134
The Loving Tree	136
Regret	138
The Day I Buried Old Blue	140
An Old Man Goes Home	142
The Legend of Old Jake	144
Repayment	146
The Thing in the Peterson Place	148
Everything in Its Season	151
Cousin Charley Guards the Chickens	152
About the Author	154

FOREWORD

I guess there is an inner need in everyone to hear a good story. From the time when our ancestors hunkered down around a fire and listened to the old ones speak of a long ago buffalo hunt or battles over hunting grounds, down through the ages to our own time with mass communication, like radio, TV, and the Internet, the teller of tales is in demand.

America is a land where tales of the old country and the sea have been passed down from generation to generation. Ethereal phantoms travel through the mountains of Kentucky and Tennessee, while out west they say the ghosts of Wyatt Earp and Doc Holliday still stalk the streets of Tombstone, waiting for their meeting at the O.K. Corral to once more confront the Clantons and McClaurys.

Myself, I've always felt, in the deepest recesses of my being, that I have a story to tell; and, if the reader can enjoy these tales by spending a quiet evening curled up in front of the fireplace with his family, then the writer will be well repaid.

Chapter 1

Cowboys and Miners

Go to any state in the west and you'll find them towns that just dried up and withered away when their reason for being was gone. But the ghosts persist.

GHOST TOWN

Just a few crumblin' buildings, nothing much to see,
Where once people lived and loved.
Now only desolation and, once in a while, a tree.
Home now to the drifting tumbleweeds
And over all, the eternal wind,
Sighing and moaning down the dusty street.
And here and there a crumbling wall where once a house had been.

When I rode in 'twas the spring of '84,
Looking for a drink and a shave and supplies at the store.
The saloon was in desolation, the barber long since gone.
And the wind passing through the gables sang a forgotten song.

In the saloon, a few bottles unbroken. A mirror still polished behind the bar.
A picture of a pretty girl and, on the mahogany, a tarnished star.
Somehow, I felt an outsider, an unwanted intruder. And I felt almost afraid,
For only memories played there and maybe, after dark, a lonely shade.

For this town had died. Who knew the reason why?
Maybe the mines had closed, cattle drives didn't come, or the railroad
    passed it by.
The West is full of such places, remnants of another time,
Where the land would soon reclaim them. If you looked close, you could
    see the signs:
Crumbling foundations slowly becoming dust
Fight hard to keep from disappearing; but, in the end, they must.

After dark I spread my blankets in the jail. It was the only one with roof
    intact.
And I laughed at myself as I took my six gun from my pack,
For what I would face here was not of flesh and bone,
Not to be destroyed by such a weapon, for the residents sleep beneath
    the stones.

FROM THE PEN OF BIG IRV LAMPMAN

Sometime in the night I awakened from my rest
And could not get back to sleep tho' I tried my best.
Then from somewhere down the street, the sound of revelry echoed clear,
And the sound of a forgotten melody played just loud enough for me to hear.

Then the sound of girlish laughter came from down the street,
And I saw the shadow of a man fall across moonbeams at my feet.
And then I heard a shot that I knew was fired long ago,
And the sound of a body falling. Once again, he'd been too slow.

Only once he'd hesitated. Conscience had stayed his hand.
And he paid the price of his mistake as he shed his life's blood in the sand.
And now his ghost stops to nod to me, as he passes his way alone
To beat the first rays of dawning home, for he sleeps beneath the stones.
Yes, it was just a ghost town. Soon it would be no more.
Just a few crumbling buildings with bullet holes in the floor.

But I won't forget what I saw that night.
And I won't forget the sounds.
Like whispers from another time, crying lonesome in the wind,
There in that ghost town.

WHEN DEATH CAME A-RIDIN' A HORSEBACK

Now he was an old puncher, tough as they come.
He was a graduate of the school of hard knocks,
Used to the ways of knuckles and guns.
And he never ran away from anything, but it was plain he was scared to death.
Fear stood out on his time-worn face,
And you could hear it on his ragged breath.
His eyes bugged out and his hands shook
As he tried to hold a coffee cup to his lips.
His hand kept reaching down for reassurance to brush the gun at his hip.
We all stood huddled around the campfire like a bunch of scared kids;
And, if the truth be known, we weren't much more.
I guess I was about seventeen or so,
But I'd been on a drive up from Texas to Abilene, my first, the year before.
And I'd faced rustlers and stampedes and once an old grizzly came roarin' around.
But, with a little luck and a Forty Four Forty, I'd put that old outlaw down.
But this was different 'cause something had scared that old fella nigh outta his wits,
And I figured he was a lot more trail-wise than I'd ever be.
And the way he kept watchin' the dark beyond the fire sure scared the hell outta me.
When he finally managed to talk he said, "Boys, this is my last drive.
I'll never go out again 'cause tonight I met old Death himself out there,
A horseback a-flashin' his God-awful grin.
The horse he was ridin' was nothing but hooves and hide,
But I'll never forget his haunted eyes,
Terrified by that thing on his back.
And I felt terrible sorry for that poor tormented critter;
And, if I could have held a gun, I'd a shot him and that's a fact.
It would have been a mercy, but I was shakin'
So I was afraid something was gonna fly off. I ain't ashamed of it,
And I ain't a-sayin' I ain't a-wishin' this drive was over, but I never been known to quit."

Well, we'd finally settled down and had just turned in
When this awful cry made us start up out of our blankets in fear.
It was a horse in mortal terror, and it was the worst sound I hope I'll ever hear.
And then this awful stench came floatin' on the wind,
And there's no mistakin' that smell.

FROM THE PEN OF BIG IRV LAMPMAN

It was the smell of Death, and then there was that cry again.
It was awful. That's the only way to describe it,
Like that poor old critter had just escaped from Hell
And was bein' pulled back bit by bit.
And then, boys, outta the dark and up to our fire,
Came staggering a terrible sight.
Three or four of the fellas took off a-runnin',
And I would have if I hadn't a been paralyzed with fright.
For here was a poor old bronc, barely able to stagger,
And tied on his back was a long dead man, takin' his last ride.
A rope went around under the horse's belly,
And to the saddle horn his hands were tied.
God only knows how long the horse had been carryin' his terrible burden.
A long time judging by the shape they both was in.
But how the man got tied onto the horse's back?
To guess that, boys, I couldn't begin.
The poor old pony whickered to us, as if to say,
"Please get him off my back."
And when we did, that poor old critter just collapsed by the fire
And died right there in his tracks.
Well, me, I'd seen a dead man before
So at least the fear was gone.
And I tried to make out I hadn't been scared at all,
That I'd figured it was somethin' like that all along.

Now here in my warm cabin by a roarin' fire,
Listenin' to the coyotes cry out their woes to the moon,
I think of that night Death came ridin'
Up to our fire out of that dark as black as the tomb.
Don't kid yourself. If you'd a been there,
You'd a been as scared as me.
'Cause when Death came a-ridin a horseback
It was a terrible thing to see.

THE MEN WITH THE TIED-DOWN GUNS

They came riding in out of the desert
Keeping their backs to the sun.
Seven grim men with their hats pulled low,
Each with a tied-down gun.

The dogs ran out in a noisy chorus,
Then one by one they slunk away.
Even the dogs could tell they weren't like other men.
Tonight there'd be hell to pay.

They sat their horses at the end of the street,
Quietly checking the town.
They sat like seven angels of death
Making neither move nor sound.

The horses they rode were, from the first to the last,
All a giant of the breed,
All black as the raven's wing,
All huge and powerful steeds.

They moved as one to the front of the saloon,
Each move like a well-oiled machine.
Hands dangled close to the tied-down guns,
Each man hard-eyed and mean.

And each of us wondered what they'd come for,
These men with the tied-down guns.
We all asked the question in the back of our minds,
Am I the reason they've come?

All afternoon they sat in the saloon,
Each with his back to the wall,
Watchin' every move in the place,
Seein' if one of us would "open the ball."

The leader of the bunch was the biggest of all,
At least six foot five or more.
He spoke not a word, and only his eyes moved,
Watchin' the windows and doors.

FROM THE PEN OF BIG IRV LAMPMAN

His face was cold and hard,
His eyes glittered under his hat.
Only the devil himself on his throne in hell
Ever had a look like that.

The heat hung over the street like a shroud so hot
It threatened to bludgeon you dumb.
Mothers kept the kids in off the street
Fearing, at nightfall, death would come.

And you know there was some kinda smell hung in the air,
Kinda like a fog filling the skies,
Felt like it could almost choke off your breath,
The smell of it burning your eyes.

Kinda like black powder smoke,
But somehow stronger still.
Down in the street everything was quiet as death,
The sun sunken behind the hills.

The preacher called us into the church;
And, boy, the place was full to the doors.
The seats were full and so were the aisles,
Children crouching on the floor.

And Benny the Drunk vowed never to drink again—
Not even to help his cough.
And Tommy Steele, the town's tough kid,
Dropped his gun in the water trough.

Men shook hands with their neighbors,
Forgetting disagreements they'd had before.
And a man wanted for twenty years came up
At the jailhouse door.

As the clock on the courthouse struck
Making us almost jump out of our skins.
Making us feel it was the stroke of doom,
The preacher led us in prayer again.

And while we sat there in the church,
Waiting for hell to start out in the street,

▶

The fires of perdition feeling so close
We could almost feel the heat.

Then the sound of galloping hoofbeats
Headed for the edge of town.
Seven men on seven horses headed away.
What a beautiful sound!

Then the preacher started chucklin' down deep in his chest,
And all the rest of us joined in,
Slapping our knees and wiping our eyes,
The town coming alive again.

And the smell of fire and brimstone
No longer burned our eyes.
The moon rose in majestic beauty
Into a cloudless sky.

Who were they that visited us
On that day so long ago?
Were they lawmen? Were they outlaws?
Nobody seemed to know.

But they sure made a change in our town,
These men with the tied-down guns.
Were they visitors from Heaven or a warning from Hell?
Nobody knew from whence they'd come.

Benny died as sober as a judge,
An old, old man who no longer had his cough.
And for years afterward you could see a rusted six gun
At the bottom of the water trough.

Well, boys, you ask me if this story's true.
Damn right, I was there
When the devil sat on a barstool.
Fire and brimstone filled the air.

The church filled up for the very first time
When they came riding in out of the sun.
Everyone of us breathed a lot easier when they left,
These men with the tied-down guns.

FROM THE PEN OF BIG IRV LAMPMAN

BORN A HUNDRED YEARS TOO LATE

Never before, or never again hereafter, has our country, or any country, known
    such a time as the frontier, the western expansion of the United States.
From the day the first long hunter crossed over the Appalachians, it was a land
    of passion over unbounded hates.
Where else could a man come across towns with names like Tombstone,
    Dodge City, Hard Times, Dry Wells, named for a dozen reasons, in a
    dozen ways?
And, men like Wild Bill Hickok, Billy the Kid, and Doc Holliday?
It was a county built with hard work, vision, horses, cattle and guns,
Of a living eked out of the mountains, or gold dug out under burning
    desert suns.
And, what a land! Mountains so high you could walk right up and touch the
    face of God,
Or prairies, lush and green, where the plow had never broken the sod.
Air, fresh and pure. Water so clean and fresh you could drink from the stream
    of hundreds of springs, gushing forth like a gift from God.
The rivers running down the canyons, making the mountains ring.
But, we must never forget that people were here first.
Men with names like Sitting Bull, Crazy Horse, and Gall
From the mountains, prairies, and plains they came to answer the battle call.
And to preserve their way of life, they fought terribly, at places like Adobe
    Walls, Wagon Box, and the Little Big Horn.
They fought hard and long; but, in the end, they lost.
The squaws sang the death song. Yes, never again will we see the like.
It was a time like no other, for those who had true grit.
As for me, I feel a twinge of regret. I'm sorry I missed it.
Not long ago, I stopped in one of those western towns and felt it drawing
    me, too.
And at Boot Hill I read the stone put up for a poor unfortunate, hung by
    mistake in 1882.
And, someone with a caustic sense of humor from so many years before
Wrote, "Here lies Les Moore, four slugs from a forty-four. No less, no
    Moore."
Yes, here they all lie together: rancher, cowboy, gambler, gunfighter, all trying
    for their chance at fame,
And, be it by stampede, thirst, snakebite, arrow, or bullet, in the end, it is still
    the same.
No matter. I'm resigned to it. It will be my fate:
Born in the twentieth century, over a hundred years too late.

WHY

Now, the ants are a-bitin', but I dasn't scratch.
Can't afford a luxury like that.
My throat is dry from a terrible thirst.
It's one hundred and ten, but that ain't the worst.
'Cause out there, somewhere, is a man with a gun.
White or red, one of us will be dead 'fore this day is done.
I'll fight to the death, and I'll never give in.
And I'll blow his head off if he comes snoopin' again.

A deer jumps up out in the brush.
Sneakin' in on his belly, sure is a crafty cuss.
Eight hours gone and I ain't seen hide or hair,
Just bullets buzzin' by. He's out there somewhere,
But I don't know where.

Now, a rattler crawls up and stops at my boot.
I break out in a sweat, but I dasn't shoot.
He rattles his warnin' and darts his tongue,
And he don't know he's starin' down the barrel of my gun.
If you die of a bullet or snake bite, you're just as dead,
Venom through your veins or a bullet through your head.
To hell with that snake, don't make a sound.
Make the wrong move and you'll be under the ground.
Now, there's a buzzard. That's one thing I hate.
He'll win in the long run. He's patient. He can wait.
I wonder if my antagonist is gone. It's been three hours without a trace.
I decide to take a peek, and a heavy slug kicks sand in my face.
It glances off a rock with a banshee whine.
It dang near got me for the second time.
Nope, he's still there. No doubt about that.
There's a quarter-sized hole through the brim of my hat.
I fire back for good measure. I never knew a day could be so long.
Another slug goes by a-singin' its song.

FROM THE PEN OF BIG IRV LAMPMAN

The sun continues on its journey across the sky.
And, for the hundredth time, I ask myself, "WHY?"
If it's my horse he's after, why doesn't he just take it and go?
Is it somethin' personal? God only knows,
Though I've never touched a thing that didn't belong to me.
Well, the sun will be down in an hour or so.
Will he leave then? I don't know.

A sage hen takes off in flight.
Is he movin' closer? Dang right!
Now, the horse ain't been spooked that I can see.
The gold's in his grasp, so what he's after is me.
The waves of heat drains drops of moisture from this barren land.
The ants have been feastin' on me for eight hours or more,
Ever since this mornin' when he started this war.
I don't understand, as hard as I try,
As I ask myself over and over, "WHY?"
My shirt's soaked with sweat. My throat's dry as a bone.
He ain't quittin' and neither am I. One of us will leave here alone,
And one of us will lie dead here on the sand
To become a permanent resident of this harsh land.

A river of sweat runs down my back.
It's been a long day, and that's a fact.
But at last the day's over, and the moon rises into the sky.
I hear him movin' closer out there in the brush.
When he could get away, he keeps coming. WHY?
Suddenly, he's there at the wagon, and he slips and falls over a can of
    axle grease.
Then the rifles are hammerin' and yammerin', speakin' their piece.
My slugs hit him and smash him down,
And a minute later, he lies dead on the ground.
I've never seen him before. What was he after?
He didn't want the gold or the horse.
The moon shakes his head up there in the sky.
And for the rest of my days, I'll wonder, "WHY?"

THE LAST OF THE BREED

We stood there in the street like two old bulls facin' our last hurrah,
Two remnants of a bygone day, two of the biggest fools you ever saw.
For the rest of our kind was long dead, or grown old and were fadin' away.
For some real or imagined insult, in a second, one would die and one would be the last survivor of a violent and bloody day.

The first horseless carriages were coughin' and wheezin' their way down the street of our town;
And electric lights had replaced the gaslights, and they lit the streets about as bright as day after the sun went down.

Now, back years ago, they used to say I was one of the best; and, I guess, he was, too.
As the years went by, our kind had dwindled to just two.
I stood there wishin' I was someplace else, then it was too late. His hand blurred and came up with his gun.
Though I don't remember drawin', I felt my gun buck in my hand; and, after a second of roarin' thunder, I still stood there and he lay in the street. The terrible deed was done.

Well, that was a long time ago, now ten years or more.
And after that day, it was never the same. I wasn't the man I'd been before.
Now I water the flowers on his grave. I'm sure he would've done the same for me.
Now my wife is gone; and, at last, there is only me.

So, old friend, when we meet up there I wonder what we will find to say.
Maybe we will go fishin' or somethin'. Hell, we never needed those damn guns anyway.

FROM THE PEN OF BIG IRV LAMPMAN

STARFIRE: WE WON'T SEE HIS LIKE AGAIN

On the high plains, they called him Starfire, and we'll not see his like again:
His coat blue black as the darkest night, his speed like the mountain wind.
His eyes flamed with unquenchable fire, on his forehead a diamond of purest white.
They say he would run for the joy of it alone in the prairie night.

In those times, any cowboy would have given a year's wages to get a rope on him, but it was not to be.
He could show his heels to the fastest horses so he remained untouchable, runnin' free.
Almost without number are the legends they tell about him.
The mightiest of a mighty breed, and we'll not see his like again.

At first, it was thought he was but a legend, one of the stories the Indians told.
For that was the time when a great horse was almost idolized, and many great ones were bought and sold.
Why? I don't know. But I alone was chosen. And, out there on a cold and moonlit night,
I saw the mighty Starfire, and I'll never forget the sight:
A great black horse, the starlight dancin' off his coat,
His nostrils flarin' and mane a-flyin', fire flashin' from his eyes as black as sin.
I thank God I was chosen, for we'll not see his like again.

But that was many years ago. My youth, like the eagle, now has flown.
Starfire like all his breed is gone now, and I am left alone.
But the legends go on about a giant black horse, a ghost racin' the mountain wind.
All I know is that there never was such a horse, and we'll not see his like again.

CONFRONTATION

He towered there in the trail
Barely forty yards away,
A scarred old veteran of many a battle,
King of all he surveyed.

He stood there, a primeval beast
From the dim reaches of a long ago time.
His hide bore the marks of many a fight,
Some with his kind and, I'm sure, some with mine.

Twelve feet and fifteen hundred pounds,
He stood there testin' the wind.
His head swingin' from side to side,
And he roared out his challenge again.

A sad regret gripped my heart
As I eased the hammer off the cap.
The beads of sweat moistened my brow
Up under the brow of my hat.

For my skill with the rifle I held in my hands,
I knew was next to none.
But I didn't want to harm him.
I didn't want to use my gun.

Our meetin' that day was the purest chance.
I'm sure he meant no harm to me.
For my part, I fervently wished to be someplace else.
There were lots of places I'd rather be.

Then I knew he had my scent.
Any second the charge could come.
So I centered the rifle on a spot on his breast,
His yellow hide glistenin' in the sun.

FROM THE PEN OF BIG IRV LAMPMAN

Suddenly I saw a flicker
Of understandin' come into his eyes.
I nodded to him; and, I swear, he nodded to me.
Somehow as he prepared for battle, he saw compassion in my eyes.

The two of us stood, eyein' each other,
Both tryin' to find a way out of there.
I started to ease back down the trail,
His poppin' of teeth chilled my blood, his roarin' prickled my hair.

Then as suddenly as it came,
The danger was past.
For, with one more roar for good measure
And with many a backward glance,
He turned and ambled away.
As for me, I broke all records, beatin' a hasty retreat.
God had smiled on us both that day.

As many years have come and gone,
I'm sure the king is gone.
Thank God it didn't come to teeth and claws
Or a bullet to decide who was right or wrong.

When his time came, he was up in the mountains,
Livin' as the grizzly has since the dawn of time.
Though it might have been a bullet that killed the king,
Thank God it wasn't mine.

THE DEVIL HORSE

Now, he was nothin' but fifteen hundred pounds of trouble
Wrapped up in a whip leather bag.
He'd bite you every chance he got.
Just saddlin' him would leave a wrangler limp as a rag.

He'd wrinkle up his upper lip
And show long, yellow teeth in a kind of hideous grin.
Anybody lucky enough to get off his back in one piece
Never climbed board again.

He'd busted up every rider I had on the place
One time or another.
I guess anyone of them would gladly herd snakes
Than try to ride him if they had their druthers.

One look in those evil eyes would make your hair stand up.
There was no doubt this bronco was clear insane.
I'd finally made up my mind, the best for all concerned,
Was for me to put a bullet right through that evil brain.

Fact is, I'd gone into the house for my rifle,
Figured everybody would be better off once the deed was done.
When, up the road, a stranger came ridin' and
He looked like the toughest man under the sun.

His eyes were tiny blue chips of steel. His face was like old harness leather
Soaked in brine, then dried under a prairie sun.
His hands were just as hard, showin' the marks of years of work,
And at his leg hung a tied-down gun.

You could see this old boy had been down the river and over the mountain
And "give" was a word he didn't know.
He'd ride a horse into hell and stoke the furnace
Just to watch the glowin' coals.

"Word has it you have a horse to ride,"
He said in a voice as dry as a prairie wind.
"I'll ride him to a standstill, make no mistake, but
I don't bother 'less they're mean as sin."

FROM THE PEN OF BIG IRV LAMPMAN

Well, the boys all heard him, and they all gathered 'round
Just to watch the fun.
They don't miss a trick when he walked up to the fence and
Took off the tied-down gun.

It took three men, but he finally put on the blinds,
And they stood back while he climbed on.
When we dropped the blinds, that devil horse exploded,
And I'll never know how he stayed on.

That old horse was a-pitchin' and squealin'
And twistin' like a mocassin snake.
His hooves strikin' sparks, his eyes flashin' fire,
Every jump a-screamin' his hate.

Then he started sunfishin',
Turnin' his belly up to the sun.
Then headin' straight for the fence to smash
The hated thing on his back off in a boundin' run.

The stranger stuck on his back like a burr,
Not givin' at all.
Then the evil bronco reared up and fell on his back
Tryin' to crush the rider in the fall.

But the stranger was off to the side,
Then came up still aboard rakin' the old devil with his spurs.
His curses, mingled with the horse's shrieks,
Still stuck on his back like a burr.

Sweat ran like a river
Under that relentless sun.
Dust swirled around horse and man,
But the battle had only begun.

You know, all at once, I noticed there wasn't a sound outside the fence.
We were watchin' a ride beyond belief.
Slowly came a buildin' respect for both man and beast,
And a fear that they'd come to grief.

▶

For, a poundin' like that couldn't go on,
Something had to give.
For, make no mistake, somethin' would break,
And maybe only one would live.

Slowly, almost imperceptibly at first,
The devil horse began slowin' down.
The jumps became smaller, and the squeals became less;
And, finally, the old warrior came to a standstill,
His sides heavin' and his breath comin' in sobbin' gasps.
A mighty cheer sounded loud and long—
The devil horse had been rode at last.

The stranger collected his money, and I asked his name.
Told him I had plenty of work if he cared to stick.
He flashed me a wicked grin and said, "No! And, by the way,
Everybody calls me Old Nick."

FROM THE PEN OF BIG IRV LAMPMAN

TEN THOUSAND ON THE PROD

Now, I've heard the wind in the mountain passes
Howl like a thing gone mad.
I've heard its sighin' and moanin' around a campfire at night
When we were dead broke, and coffee was all we had.

I've heard a lobo wolf at night and
The sound of a plow as it broke the sod.
But the most fearful sound in the world
Is the cry, "Stampede!" and ten thousand on the prod.

Now, a cow is a mighty skittish critter.
Sometimes almost anything can set them off:
A flicker of lightnin', a rag caught on a bush, or
The jingle of a bridle at the water trough.

For, when a herd is runnin', it's a thing devoid of reason,
Washin' over the prairie like an unstoppable ocean tide.
I've seen what was left of a cow camp on the prairie
Where every man died.

I've seen Saint Elmo's Fire out there,
Dancin' on a sea of horns.
I've had to shoot many a good pony,
Hooked and gutted, bloody, ragged and torn.

I remember one night, many years ago,
Something had been buildin' all day,
Hot and miserable as only days on the trail can be.
A herd can get mighty hard to manage when the weather gets that way.

Off to the west you could see storm clouds
Rearin' their ugly heads.
And I could feel a pricklin' at the nape of my neck
To fill my soul with dread.

The night hawks were out circlin' the herd,
Singin' those longhorns a lullaby.
Sometimes it seems to help quiet those half-wild critters,
Though God only knows why.

Then, suddenly, softly at first,
We could hear the wind begin to sigh. ▶

A minute later the thunder was rollin',
And the lightnin' slashed the sky.

I'd just got through cussin' our luck and
Wonderin' what could be worse.
A second later I had my answer
With a dropped coffee cup and the sound of a muffled curse.

Just like that the herd was on its feet.
A second later they'd started to run.
As I ran for my horse I breathed a prayer
That nobody would die before this night was done.

I vaulted into the saddle—
I could do that in those days—
And spurred my pony after the leaders.
That's the time for a cowboy to earn his pay.

I could see a horse off to my left
When the lightnin' flashed,
A cowled figure on a great black horse,
And he flashed me a grin as he flew past.

Yes, old Death himself was prowlin' out there
In that night as black as sin.
For I'd seen him out there abreast of me,
And he flashed me his terrible grin.

If he had his way, I had no doubt, man and beast
Would both go down under the herd, dyin' bloody and torn.
For Death waited there under the hooves
Or hooked upon the horns.

I drew my gun and slipped the hammer,
Firin' as fast as I could.
I yelled and yipped as loud as I could,
Though I feared it would do no good.

The thunder rolled and boomed and
Lightnin' split the sky.
The rain came down in the unendin' sheets.
We had little chances of savin' the herd, but we got paid to try.

FROM THE PEN OF BIG IRV LAMPMAN

And out there in the night,
The cowled figure waved and grinned in glee.
He waved and grinned out there in the storm
And shook his scythe at me.

Now, in those days, every herd had a leader,
And we call it the "Judas steer" 'cause they led the others right to the slaughter pen.
Every one had his own markings
And was well-known by all the men.

That night what I saw leading the herd
Wasn't our Judas steer.
It was a great black beast with blood-red eyes,
And he filled my heart with fear.

Steam rolled off his back,
And he bellowed his challenge into the wind.
I figured he'd lead this herd straight to hell,
Still pursued by the men.

All it takes is your horse steppin' in a prairie dog hole
Or stumbling in his headlong run to lay you in a grave beneath the sod.
Even brave men blanch in fear
When there's ten thousand on the prod.

Slowly they began to run themselves out,
Finally coming to a circling run,
And then to a walk.
The stampede was finally done.

We buried three good men the next morning.
Death had claimed his own.
We read over them and marked their graves
And left them there alone.

Yes, I've heard and seen some mighty strange things
In my lifetime spent in the West:
Thunder and lightnin' and bawling cattle.
But I can't remember anything like that night, though I've tried my best.

Well, the big drives are only a memory now
Since the farmers came to break the sod.
But they'll never see what I lived through that night
With ten thousand on the prod.

OLD HIGGINS

Now, I knew him as Old Higgins,
And we could see he was rough as a hickory briar,
Born and raised in the mountains,
Tempered by wind and fire.

He was a quiet and peaceful man
Who just wanted to work his land.
He was the kind of man it took to settle this country.
Old Higgins was a mountain man.

Now, he hunted with us boys
When deer season rolled around.
And he'd kill extra deer and take the meat
To the needy of our town.

He carried a huge old mountain gun,
Fifty caliber, at least, I guess.
Of all the men I knew who grew up with guns—
All dead shots—Old Higgins was the best.

I remember the time the Carson boys
Picked a fight with him one night.
He just walked out to his horse and walked back in
To stand in the tavern's lights.

He'd buckled on an old revolver,
In his eyes was an icy chill.
Not a man in the tavern that night ever doubted that
Old Higgins had come to kill.

They'd cussed him and put their hands on him,
And one of them spit in his face.
I guess they'd figured they'd made a mistake
When it got deathly quiet in the place.

He stood there like a curly old wolf,
Fangs bared and ready to fight.
His old gray eyes glittered like pieces of glass,
Hard in the lantern light.

FROM THE PEN OF BIG IRV LAMPMAN

The toughest of those two just went to pieces,
Sweat popped out on his face.
They started backin' toward the door,
And I knew they were starin' death in the face.

I swear the temperature had dropped twenty degrees.
In the room was a terrible chill.
Everybody knew if they made one wrong move
Those boys would die. Old Higgins drew to kill.

Well, the Carsons left town after that,
But the fight was talked about over and over again.
Old Higgins went back to his farm,
And he was never bothered again.

Oh, we heard stories about him,
And the gunman he used to be.
But I never took much stock in stories.
He was always a friend to me.

Come to think of it, I never saw a speck of dust on his rifle
Or that old six gun he kept hangin' by the door.
But I never heard him brag, not even once,
About the man he'd been before.

We found him dead one morning by the fire, in his chair,
Looking at something none of us could see.
But his rifle was primed and ready,
And he was smiling, or so it seemed to me.

On the table by his hand, held there
By a finger cold and dead,
Were two words that I understood:
"Goin' West," is what they said.

And, somehow, I know Old Higgins is back in the mountains.
He's found his heaven, as I hope I'll find mine.
But I wouldn't fit in with him up in the Rockies.
Old Higgins was one of a kind.

THE MYSTERIOUS KILLER
of CAUFIELD COUNTY

The winter had set in early
That year on the high plains.
My Dad said it was about the earliest he could remember,
And most of the old timers said the same.

Oh, we were luckier than most I guess.
Least we'd managed to get in a mow full of hay for the stock.
Good thing, too, 'cause it snowed for three days and nights
Till it finally quit about four in the mornin', I saw by Ma's store-bought clock.

I had the coffee goin' by the time
I heard Dad stirrin' around.
It was just gettin' light, and I could see
We had about two feet of snow on the ground.

After we'd had breakfast, we started out to feed the stock,
But I just had a feelin' that something wasn't right.
As soon as I saw the door to the hog house,
I knew we'd had a visitor durin' the night.

Now, I never was one to keep hogs around,
But Dad set store by them.
Said a man would always have bacon when he needed it and
Could help pay the bills so every couple of months he'd sell a few of them.

Only he wouldn't be sellin' any this month 'cause whatever had gotten in
Had left the hogs all torn to pieces, scattered all over dead.
Dad just looked sick, standin' there with glazed eyes,
Scratchin' his head.

Old Rounder, our bear hound, came roarin' in the door,
Stopped cold in his tracks, let out a howl, and took off for other parts.
Now I never seen that dog act like that before.
Seemed like he was whipped before he could start.

Not that I wasn't feelin' a might skittish myself
'Cause whatever it was didn't leave tracks like any I'd seen before.
And he'd come through that shed like he hadn't even slowed down
For a heavy barred oaken door.

FROM THE PEN OF BIG IRV LAMPMAN

I checked the load in my gun
And put on a fresh cap.
I wished I had one of those new repeaters Dad had told me about,
But I couldn't afford nothin' like that.

Well, as I was sayin', whatever came callin' last night had left a track as big as a grizzly,
But no grizzly ever had a smell like that thing had.
All through the hog house and out in the yard, it just reeked.
It got to me, and I know it did to Dad.

I tracked the thing up the valley about four or five miles.
That was about as far as I could get and still make it back by dark, so I started back.
Truth is, if I was bein' honest, I wasn't lookin' forward to meetin' up
With that critter after dark—and that's a fact.

That night after supper while we were sittin' around smokin' our pipes,
I asked Dad what he thought it might be. Well, sir, he just shook his head.
Something he'd never run across before in this county after
Forty years of hunting and fishing was all he said.

I'd boarded up the barn and the hog shed with oak logs.
And it must have worked 'cause those big tracks was all around.
But at least it hadn't gotten in to do any more killin'.
But what bothered me most was I hadn't heard a sound.

The sky was overcast so I couldn't see anything by moonlight,
But I knew it was out there, Heaven knows.
I got the message clear as a written paper,
And it came to me through my nose.

Man, that thing stunk. It was so bad it just choked off your breath.
It must have seemed twice as bad to old Rounder.
We had to throw him outside to do his business,
And he'd come back scared to death.

Well, nothin' much happened for about three weeks until one night I'd gone down to the smokehouse to get one of our last slabs of bacon, when all of a sudden the hairs on the back of my neck stood up, and I just kinda got cold all over 'cause something was watchin' me through the window.
I couldn't see too much except these two big glowin' eyes,
And I sure felt sick 'cause they were about seven feet off the ground. ▶

There was no mercy in those eyes, no hatred, just the cold look of
    the carnivore.
I knew nothin' stood between me and eternity but that flimsy smokehouse door.
All this time it never made a sound.
I was cussin' myself for being every kind of a fool
For comin' out without my gun
'Cause I knew if that critter came for me
I was done.

It just stood there, this big, ugly black shape with that awful smell just starin'
    at me, and me
Swearin' to whoever might be listenin' I'd never come outside without my
    rifle again.
Then it kinda wrinkled its lips up off its teeth;
And, boy, it was ugly as sin.

We stood there a few minutes that seemed like hours
'Cause I figured I'd had it, and then the thing just ambled away.
I took off for the house like a scalded cat, and when I got inside
I made up my mind that's where I was gonna stay

At least 'til daylight. Then I took my rifle and went out to where the thing
    had stood.
Sure enough, I found where it had circled around and came up on the cabin.
Who knows what the thing had in mind, but it had circled around
And circled around tryin' to find a way to get in.

Well, the months dragged by
As they always do in the winter on the high plains.
Nothin' much to do but take care of the stock
And watch and wait for the first spring rain.

I'd almost figured our visitor had moved on till one night I came home
And found Ma and Dad boarded up in the living room with a shotgun full
    of buckshot for company.
Ma said she'd been out to the clothesline and somethin' just told her to look
    around; and
There was a big, ugly, dark shape watchin' her back in the shadows, makin'
    it hard to see.

FROM THE PEN OF BIG IRV LAMPMAN

She had backed toward the house and hollered for Dad and he'd got
    her inside.
They'd been there ever since, waitin' for me to get home.
Dad was white as a sheet, but I reminded him the thing hadn't hurt anybody
    yet;
And, with that big Greener ten-gauge, they weren't exactly alone.

I figured we all needed a change of scenery so next day I hitched up
    the team,
And we headed into town for supplies.
Truth is, I had about as bad a case of cabin fever I'd ever had.
And, by the way they were actin', so did Ma and Dad.

You know, I found out at the saloon that we weren't the only ones
    to lose stock
To the Gouger, as we'd took to callin' him, by the way he tore up his kills.
People had been findin' dead cattle all over these hills.
I asked old Tom Fun Maker, the Indian medicine man,
What he thought it was when he came in for tobacco.
He said the Indians had known about the things for years, and
They were bad medicine. Where they came from he didn't know.

Bad medicine? I guess so! He didn't have to tell me.
I still remember that night at the smokehouse
With those eyes seven feet off the ground and starin' straight at me.
One of the Olson boys said he'd found
Where some of those big tracks led into a cave, so he followed them in.
He didn't find the Gouger, but what he did find he said would make him
    think long and hard
Before he followed those tracks into a cave again.

He said he'd found what was left of a big, old mountain cat just
    torn to pieces.
He said that old painter cat had gone two hundred pounds and didn't
    stand a chance.
That thing had just torn him apart. The Olson boy said he was so scared
    he wasn't ashamed to
Admit it. He dang near wet his pants.

▶

He didn't have to tell me not to follow the thing into no cave.
I'd known that right from the start.
Anything could carry off a two hundred pound hog could tear a man apart.
Well, nothin' much happened for the rest of the winter.

We knew the thing was around though
'Cause every so often that stench would come floatin' on the wind.
Up till now the Gouger hadn't hurt anyone,
But all that changed one day when the sheriff came ridin' in.

Said the Gouger was around again.
This time was different though 'cause this time the thing had killed old
    Charlie Sims.
Said they'd found the old man and his dog just torn to pieces up at his place,
And the whole town was stirred up feelin' mean as sin.

He said he was gettin' up a posse and wanted me to go along. So after gettin'
    Ma and Dad set up in town, we rode out about sunup; and a madder,
    more determined, bunch you never saw.
Charlie had been a well-liked fella, and everyone of us wanted to nail that
    thing's hide to a barn door. But after five days of pokin' through caves
    and climbin' over cliffs, we had to give up. That thing sure made fools
    of the Law.

But the strangest thing was,
The Gouger disappeared as mysteriously as it came.
No more tracks were found. No more cattle killed. Nothin'.
Dad said it was a doggone shame.
Not only did the thing get away with killin' old Charlie,
But because we didn't kill it, we wouldn't know for sure if it would ever be
    back.
Even now I remember that night in the smokehouse,
And it still gives me the creeps. That's a fact.

Well, anyway, boys, there you have it,
The story of the mysterious killer of Caufield County.
Bad medicine comes in heaps,
So go ahead and get a good night's sleep.
Throw another log on the fire; and, if you see some eyes out there in the
    dark,
And something smells bad, don't wake me. I still get the creeps.

But, you know, what's really spooky?
Who knows where the Gouger's gonna show up next?
These things can come and go as they please.
I'd sure hate to wake up with an awful smell chokin' off my breath and
With some big, ugly hands around my neck.
How about you? Who knows what the thing will do?

A VISITOR IN CAMP

Seems as how there was this bunch of fellas in a cow camp back in 1895 or so, and they'd just settled down for supper and then would be headin' for the blankets. In those days, before pickups and such, if you were a ways out from the home place, you spent the night in a camp right on the prairie. They had an older fella with them to do the cookin'; and, just as he'd served up the bacon and beans, a call came from out in the sage. "Ho the camp." At that time and place if you were approachin' a camp, the wisest thing was to sing out and announce yourself and wait for an invitation. A lot of the boys carried a saddle gun; and, when out on the range, some of them still even packed a forty-five side gun. At that time, there were still rustlers around; and any number of unsavory characters roamed the west. Nobody wanted to ride into a camp and get blown out of the saddle by some trigger-happy cowpoke.

"Ho yourself. Come on it. There's not much, but you're welcome and the coffee's hot." Well, the stranger rode in and after ground reining, hunkered down in the shadows outside the firelight. Well, they passed the time for a while, jawin' about the weather and such, and the cook had just leaned across the fire with some more bacon and beans when a little spilled onto the fire and it flared up. That old fella got a good look at the stranger's face, and you'd a thought he was going to drop dead right there. He turned as white as a sheet, his eyes bugged out, and he was gaspin' like a fish somebody had tossed on the bank.

"You. By God, it's you." And he was shakin' so bad he could barely hold the coffee pot.

Well, anyway, just like that, the stranger was gone, and "Thanks for the vittles," and then they heard him ride away.

"What in the devil's got into you?" one of the fellas asked the cook. When he could talk, he said, "You remember I told you I was workin' down in Lincoln County when that war was goin' on? Well, I got to know all them fellas pretty well. I never forget a face. And either all those witnesses made a mistake, or we just had coffee with a ghost. Boys, as sure as I'm a born sinner, that was the kid."

Well, everybody knew that Pat Garrett had killed Billy at Pete Maxwell's at Fort Sumner back in '81. This was '95. But 'til his dyin' day, when a wagon horse kicked him in the head and scrambled his brains, the cook still swore that it was Billy the Kid that rode up to their fire in '95.

An interesting postscript to the story is that in 1953 or so an old man calling himself Brushy Bill Roberts walked into the sheriff's office and gave himself up, claiming to be Billy the Kid. Well, he was about in his nineties, and some people laughed at him; and others wanted the hanging carried out that the kid had been sentenced to. I guess it scared the hell out of

FROM THE PEN OF BIG IRV LAMPMAN

the old fella 'cause he left for other parts. He didn't get far though and collapsed and died that evenin'.

But here's where the story takes a strange turn. Some reporter got a hold of a hotel register Brushy Bill had signed, and compared it with a letter the Kid had written to Lew Wallace. After comparing the two, the handwriting expert said they matched exactly.

COOKEE

Well, as far as I can recollect, after all these years, he wasn't a handsome man. Fact is, he was down right, baldface, homely. But, by God, he had character. You know, I never saw him look for trouble like so many of those wild cowboys would. After all those days on the drive, he'd go out of his way to avoid trouble if he could. But, to us folks, he was mother and father, brother and doctor. Whenever the need was there and when hard times came, be it a fight or stampede, Cookee could be counted on to do his share.

Why, I saw him sit up all night with a sick cowboy that had caught the flu or some such like. When Shorty died of the fever down on the Pecos, why, you never seen such a sight! You'd a thought it was his fault, the way Cookee carried on, kickin' and cussin' everything all night. Why, we all knew he'd done everything a body could. Shorty knew it, too; and he'd said so, if he could.

I remember one time. Oh, I guess, I was about eighteen. I got into some bad water. It wasn't long and I figured I was about done. The fact is, I'd a probably shot myself if I'd had the strength to lift a gun. I sat in the privy so long I figured I was gonna grow roots there. I allowed I'd be dead pretty quick, and, about that time, I didn't care. But I'd reckoned without Cookee. He wasn't ready to give up on me yet. He mixed up some kind of devil's brew that tasted like fire and brimstone and old socks that made me mad as I could get. But, boys, as sure as I'm a born sinner, it worked! Had me back on my feet in no time. I woke up that mornin', hungry as a spring grizzly and new saddle fine.

Now, I reckon if Cookee had any vices, it was playin' checkers. Now and again, he'd play with anybody—even the Devil, I remember him sayin'. He beat everyone of us a dozen times, but we never got tired of playin'. He'd jaw a mile a minute till you made a mistake. Then, you should have seen the old fella grin. Well, as I said afore, Cookee never looked for trouble. That didn't mean he'd turn tail. If trouble started and you needed somebody to side you, Cookee was right there without fail.

Like that time a bunch of renegades tried to make off with our remuda. They won't try that again. One of those fellas couldn't resist lookin' in the chuck wagon and found the eyes of a double barrel staring right at him. He threw his hands up and froze in that position. A ten gauge double will do that to a man. Cookee eared back those twin hammers, and I thought that horse thief was gonna die right there. But, Cookee just gave a motion with his head, and those folks dang near tore themselves apart getting out of there.

Yes, sir, Cookee was one of a kind. A kind that's not found these days, hard as stone and just as dependable. But, there's no call for a chuck wagon

From the Pen of Big Irv Lampman

cook now like the old days.

Sometimes when I'm in camp and the lightning dangles among the clouds, I think of Cookee and those days of long ago. Where he ended up, who knows. But, he was the best "pard" a man could ever ask for. If bein' honest and dependable is what it takes, why, he's up there behind heaven's golden doors. You know, I wonder if the Lord plays checkers. I'll just bet he enjoys a game; but if he don't, with Cookee up there, it'd be a doggone shame.

THE SOBBIN' KILLER OF THE KALAHARI

Now, I've heard it said that the jungles of Africa
Are the hottest place on Earth.
Well, I'm here to tell you if they're not,
The heat alone will make a man show his worth.
And at night under the stars,
With a lion grumbling out there beyond the firelight,
You try to act brave, but you can't help but strain your eyes,
For movement out there in the night.

There's that in the roar of a lion that brings all of man's primitive fears
To the forefront, the fear of the prey
Knowing that the predator waits out there and he's drawing closer;
And all you do is wait for the day.
Sure, you've got your rifle and the other fellows do, too.
But, somehow, this piece of wood and metal
Seems very inadequate if the lion comes for you.

I had come to the dark continent on a search for ivory,
White gold it was called back then.
We were searching for the elephant graveyard,
That elusive place elephants go to die,
And where the tusks are piled like cordwood,
Long dreamed about in the hearts of men.
We'd been traveling for so many days that it seemed
These jungles had no end. Just stretching on and on
Following the spoor of an old bull that we knew was dyin',
But he'd stumbled away and suddenly was gone.
But we knew that he was somewhere just up ahead
And with him riches beyond our wildest dreams.
Ivory, tons of it, just the thought, made my eyes gleam.

I was but twenty back in 1882
And full of all the fire and strength of youth, as all young men are,
I happened into an old friend one night as I stood at my favorite bar.
I hadn't seen him for a couple of years; and, after the customary hand shakin'
    and back slappin',
He asked what I had planned for the next couple years.
Well, I told him like it was, and that's when the talk of Africa came up.

FROM THE PEN OF BIG IRV LAMPMAN

I told him I was game, nothing much happening around here.
And so here I was in the deepest, darkest night I'd ever been in,
Bein' sized up for a midnight snack for a lion.
And I was actin' as brave as I could and standin' my ground.
If I did get eaten, it wouldn't be for lack of tryin'.
Well, the next morning one of the trackers picked up that old elephant's track again.
And excitement was runnin' high 'cause he was movin'
Straight as an arrow toward wherever he was goin', and our hopes soared again.
We followed all that day, gettin' closer all the time,
And his steps were getting slower and slower, and I figured he was about done.
I could see all the signs.

That night, sitting around the fire, we were already spending our fortune, as young fellas often will,
Talkin' about the travelin' we'd do, and the girl we were gonna marry, and the mansion up on the hill,
When out of the darkness, beyond the firelight, the most ungodly sound I've ever heard, started in.
The best way to describe it was sort of painful sobbing
Like a lost soul mourning for a lost love.
It would rise to crescendo, stop for a moment, then begin again.

I looked at Kasaba, our head bearer,
And I knew right then that we were in for trouble
'Cause he looked scared out of his mind.
His hands were shakin' and his eyes bugged out.
And he looked like the devil had just jumped out of the jungle or something of the kind.
Both of us fellas grabbed our rifles, and stood there staring into the night.
Whatever it was, it was circlin' us, moaning and sobbing,
And staying just outside of the firelight.

Well, none of us got a wink of sleep, and it was just breakin' day
When out of the night came this awful scream—that was all.
No sound of strugglin', nothin' else.
And in the morning one of our camp boys was gone—
Just disappeared—least that's the way it seemed. ▶

But he did leave a river of blood leading out into the jungle,
And we followed it with cocked rifles.
And we found what was left of him at eight o'clock or so.

I took one look and that was all I cared to see.
I let the other fellas look for signs whilst I stood back
With that old double rifle and watched the jungle, for God only knows,
After a while old Kasaba came over to me
Shakin' his head and talkin' to himself
Like he did when somethin' had him confused
And he was tryin' to figure it out.

I asked him to let me in on it,
And he proceeded to talk for more than ten minutes,
Tryin' to explain what it was all about. "No man eater, no sir,
Walks like no lion this chile ever see either. Kills for hate.
I think we best pack up and get out of this jungle.
Bad place. Bad medicine. More people die, just wait."

Well, for a while, I agreed with him;
And then, after I'd studied on it, I started to get mad.
Now whatever this thing was and why it hated like it did was my nevermind.
I hadn't done anything to harm it, and this trip had taken all the savings I had.
If it wanted a piece of my hide, well, it wouldn't be hard to find me,
And my old nitro express would be waitin' for whatever it had in mind.
Well, the bearer getting killed had kinda taken the wind out of our sails.
So we kinda laid up in camp for the rest of the day.
Kinda made a man cautious when somethin' like that happens.
Close to home, so to speak, and it's enough to make a man shiver
To see another fella torn up that way.

Well, I'd felt pretty brave that mornin' with the sun high in the sky.
But now it was getting dark, and who knew what the devil was waitin'
Out there in the dark ready to grab whoever happened by?
And, sure enough, that night as we sat around the fire
That God awful sobbin' and moanin' started in.
I don't know how to describe it.
It would start in a low moan, and build to a wail,
Like all the souls in Hell, then stop for a minute to start in again.

FROM THE PEN OF BIG IRV LAMPMAN

And it kept circlin' and circlin', round and round,
Looking for an opportunity to grab one of us when it could.
And the opportunities were sure to come. For we did our best to keep awake;
But, no matter how we tried to keep awake, it did no good.
Sometime near daybreak I must have nodded off.
And, all of a sudden, I woke with a start, and the fire had burnt down,
And then I realized somethin' was there behind me,
Tho' I hadn't heard a sound.
My hair was standin' up, like porcupine quills,
'Cause now I was hearin' this kind of snufflin' and heavy panting like.
And I could smell the stink of the thing, like the rotten flesh between its teeth.
I didn't dare move a whisker, and my hands around the double were
    clenched white.

Every time I moved, even the slightest bit, the thing would rumble,
And I knew that any second the charge would come.
That would be it and not one thing I could do.
I'd end up like the gun bearer out in the jungle, torn to bits.
Then I heard a twig snap. It was movin' closer,
And the sweat was runnin' down my back.
A bug was tryin' to climb into my ear, and I swear
I could feel the beast's hot breath on my neck.
I knew I'd never make it, and that's a fact.
Just then my buddy stepped out of the cook tent and hollered, "Hey, Homer!"
I heard a whoosh and a snarl and whirled to fire.
But I only got a glimpse of something huge, unbelievably huge.
And the beast was gone.
Well, right there I sat down. My legs were wobbly.
The leaves behind me were covered with stinking spittle from the thing.
And I couldn't stand up, and I couldn't even holler. I couldn't make a sound.
Death himself had almost claimed me, and a grisly death at that.
And, believe it or not, my hair was still standin' up under my hat.

Well, when I could stand, I hollered for John; and we looked for signs
And we found it not six feet behind where I'd been sittin'.
Six feet, for God's sake!
If I'd tried to turn to fire, no way I'd have made it.
I'd have been dead as last year's geraniums,
All because I hadn't been able to stay awake.

▶

But this time there were pug marks,
'Bout near as big as dinner plates, but only three.
Now, at last, it began to make some sense to me.
We had a three-legged killer, out there in the jungle,
With a mad on for anything human.
The tracks were there to see.
And this thing was cunning and used to the ways of men.
And, worst of all, it had lost its natural fear of man.
Not only had it lost its fear, but it was takin' some kind
Of twisted revenge on the thing it hated...man.

That night, as the fire burned low,
When that sobbin' and moanin' started, we were waitin'.
At least we knew it was flesh and blood and could be killed,
Not just some kind of forest devil that couldn't die.
Just spent its time hatin';
And, just about daybreak, it made its move
And came for me.
But we'd scattered some corn flakes and tin cans around.

And I whirled when I heard it.
I turned and pulled both triggers on the double,
And the flash made it plain to see. It was a lion,
But it was the biggest I'd ever seen!
The double caught it in mid-spring and smashed it down.
And, in a minute, it was still; and, after we checked out the carcass,
It was plain to see why the thing hated like it did.
Its jaw had been broken by a bullet, years ago,
And its back leg, too, had been smashed.
Somebody hadn't done his job. That's why it hated like it did.

Well, we never did find the elephant's graveyard.
I'd kinda lost my taste for Africa and returned to the States.
Of lions and elephants, I'd had my fill.
But maybe you folks would like to try.
I'm sure somebody will.
Africa's out there beckoning. But, it's not for me.
I'm just a country boy who's seen his share,
And that's all I want to be.

FROM THE PEN OF BIG IRV LAMPMAN

THE BANQUET

'Tis been said that the search for gold will change a man.
Well, it sure did us two, old Billy McQuade and me.
It turned us from the best of friends to the bitterest of foes
And took away our ability to see.

Greed can seep into your soul and poison your mind,
'Til everything else is gone.
When only the yellow stuff matters,
You lose your sense of right and wrong.

For now that the search is over,
And I've got the damnable stuff a-lyin' all around,
It really doesn't seem to matter at all,
For, here I am, only hours from death—and poor Bill's under the ground.

'Twas a late afternoon, in the middle of June,
When Billy came runnin' in,
Laughin' and screamin' at the top of his lungs,
On his face—a mile-wide grin.

He told me we'd finally struck it; and, sure enough,
There it was shinin' yella in the sun—
A whole mountain of gold, enough for a thousand lifetimes.
Our years of searchin' was done.

That very day we began our toil,
And every day the sacks of dust became more and more.
For we went at it like ones possessed.
Each day made us richer than the day before.

Then, subtly at first, I noticed a difference
In my partner, old Billy McQuade.
He talked little and laughed not at all,
And I marveled at the difference the gold had made.

For he became suspicious of my every move,
Thinkin' I was out to steal his share,
Watchin' with suspicion as I weighed every poke,
Fixin' on my face with a terrible glare.

'Til, one night, I came back from the privy,
And he put a bullet though the brim of my hat.
I poked him one, bang on the beak.
I couldn't let him get by with that.

I warned him he'd better
Never pull that gun again.
For, while he'd been a farmer, I'd used a gun more than once.
It was a fight he had no hope to win.

You know, it wasn't a week later
That poor Billy lost his fight with the urge to kill.
He went crazy mad and grabbed for his gun.
I buried him there on the hill.

The very next mornin' I loaded the mules
Leavin' only a little of the gold behind.
I know I should have taken more water;
But, I hated to leave any gold for another to find.

The desert, at that time of the year, is the devil's playground—
Sometimes a hundred and twenty in the shade.
After two days of that, the water gave out,
And I envied old Billy McQuade.

Two days later the mules went down, and I staggered on alone,
The gold on the mules forgotten.
It wouldn't buy me one day of water,
My throat as dry as a bone.

Then, at last, I could go no farther.
I'd have traded all the gold in the world for a little patch of shade.
Out there on the sand, a-grinnin' and laughin',
Was the Devil and Billy McQuade.

They pranced and laughed and slapped their knees,
In waves of glee.
They dotted the desert with mirages of cool water
Just to bedevil me.

From the Pen of Big Irv Lampman

As I lie here on the sand,
The last pokes of gold scattered there on the ground,
I look up in the sky and see some great dark birds
A-circlin' around.

And others are hurryin' to join them,
A family reunion is the only reason that I can see.
Then it hits me, the call's gone out, "Come to the banquet!"
And, the guest of honor is me.

THE LEGEND OF FINNEGAN'S WELL

Now they call this place the Devil's Caldron,
And I have to say it's rightly named.
The heat during the day hits one twenty.
One day spent out under the sun, and you're never the same.

Up there in the rocks the rattler waits,
The tarantula, and the scorpion, too.
Getting up there causes aches and pains a-plenty;
And when you do make it, rewards are way too few.

You know I've heard it said the Lord looks out for fools.
For some people, it's meant riches beyond their wildest dreams.
Some just have the Midas touch,
Least that's the way it seems.

Take, for instance, a fella named Finnegan
Who came from across the sea.
Just showed up and set out to find his fortune.
If bein' crazy was what it took to tackle the Devil's Caldron, he'd qualify,
    we all agreed.

He bought the house a drink.
Few will ever forget that day.
With a big grin spread across his Irish mug,
Announced he had come to stay.

When he said he was headed for the Devil's Caldron,
We all figured, well, that's the end of him.
Dead of thirst or critter bite
Would be the end of Finnegan.

It should have been, too, bein' it was the middle of summer,
The hottest time you'll find.
But Finnegan said it didn't matter, just loaded up his mules and struck out
    a-whistlin'.
I figured he must be out of his mind.

Now, he had a pick and shovel,
And a few cases of dynamite.
Most of us figured he wouldn't find a thing. Probably die out there.
He'd never make it. But old Joe, the hostler, said, "Who knows? He might."

FROM THE PEN OF BIG IRV LAMPMAN

Now, I don't know if you've heard anything
About our little piece of hell.
It's the driest place under the sun;
And hotter, too, so I've heard tell.
Here's how it came to be this legend of Finnegan's Well.

The deeper into those canyons he went, the hotter it got.
Even the rattler looks for shade durin' the heat of the day.
Every scorpion's got his own rock.
Even the tarantula's got sense enough to stay

Somewhere deep in the sand or dust,
Or wherever tarantulas go.
Where Finnegan figured he'd find to hole up
God only knows.

The sun burns the sand
With waves of shimmerin' heat.
You sweat out the water you drink so fast you can't keep up.
The dust devils dance by on dainty feet.

Finnegan kept at it though, scratchin' here and a-scratchin' there,
Never findin' a thing.
But he kept on a-sweatin' and a-swingin' that pick,
Makin' the canyons ring.

First the food gave out, then the water got low;
But Finnegan never gave it a second thought.
Bad mistake. For his sake,
I hoped he wouldn't get caught.

Out there without water, well,
A man just wouldn't have much hope.
But up in the cliffs went Finnegan,
Shinnyin' up a mile-long rope.

He placed some dynamite up there, figuring to bust loose some rock,
Least that was the way it was told to me.
Don't know any more about dynamitin' than he did about prospectin',
The old timers all agree.

▶

He put enough dynamite up there in the rocks to take off half the top
    of the mountain.
Yes, siree, when she let go, the blast just shook the earth.
Fact is, we felt the ground shake five miles away.
Scared the devil out of Finnegan, took off runnin' for all he was worth.
Then there was a terrible rumblin', rendin' sound,
And the dust came boiling up in a cloud you could see for miles around.

We went racin' out there, figured to give Finnegan a decent burial.
At least we'd have a story to tell.
And we did, too, 'cause out of those rocks
That make up our little piece of hell,
Came rushing a stream of cool, clear water,
Pure and sweet, into a deep natural cistern
To form a beautiful fresh, cold, clear well.

I guess Finnegan, in his quest for riches,
Had found for this country the greatest treasure of all.
He'd blasted into an underground river to form a lasting monument
For all of us there at the base of the canyon wall.

And Finnegan? Oh, he found his gold all right,
A whole mountain of it came washing down with the water, so I heard tell.
He married one of the local gals and set up housekeeping out at the edge
    of town,
Raised a dozen young 'uns, out there by Finnegan's Well.

Now you can find deer and bear, desert critters of every kind
That live in the Devil's Caldron. We still call it our little piece of hell.
But every critter, man, or beast finds life a little more bearable
Because of Finnegan's Well.

FROM THE PEN OF BIG IRV LAMPMAN

A TALE AT FIFTY BELOW

It's a stark and barren land,
This country of the endless snow.
It'll snatch your breath and turn it to ice
With the mercury at fifty below.

The husky burrows deep
To escape the wind as it blows.
The wolf howls out his woes to the homeless snows
As the temperature hovers at fifty below.

The great white bear prowls out there on the ice.
Be careful. You might look like a seal to him.
He's got to be ready with layers of fat
When the long night begins.

The Northern Lights do their dance at night
Out there across the snow.
And the glow of the stars turns night into day
With the temperature at fifty below.

To this God-forsaken land of cold in search of gold
Came my wife and I and our cherished little Sara Lee.
Snug in the pines at the edge of a lake
I built a home for my wife, our baby and me.

All winter long I ran my traps;
And, in summer, I mucked around for gold,
Clear mad for the yellow metal.
That's been the death of many a man gone north in search of gold.

It's a hard, hard land for a full-grown man,
Let alone a child of three.
But Sara seemed to take to it like a bee to honey
Or a sailor takes to the sea.

Till late one night out of a sound sleep
My wife awakened me.
She said Sara's fussing had awakened her,
And that fever gripped our Sara Lee.

▶

All the rest of that night we fought with the fire
That gripped our loved one and tortured her so.
And in the morning we started for the doctor many miles away,
The temperature at fifty below.

Then on and on, three nights and two days,
We raced on through the snow.
And every mile seemed to pass at a snail's pace.
I never knew a sled could go so slow.

Behind us there on the trail
I could almost see the hooded figure of Death,
Carrying his scythe and whipping his dogs,
Smiling at Sara's every ragged breath.

As we stopped to feed the dogs,
The stars dancing to and fro,
We caught our breath, then hurried on like the devil possessed,
The temperature still at fifty below.

When I stopped to mend a trace on that last night,
I could see the hooded figure had been gaining again.
And I cursed him with every curse word I knew,
And he answered with his terrible grin.

"You can't have her!"
I screamed to the ice and snow,
"I'll fight you with all I have
Out here at fifty below!"

And on and on we raced,
My heart almost bursting in my chest.
Every glance behind made the icy grip of terror
Clutch wildly at my breast.

At ten p.m. we raced into town,
The winner of a race we had to win.
And behind us the hooded figure still pursued,
And he waved and flashed his ghastly grin.

FROM THE PEN OF BIG IRV LAMPMAN

All that day and into the night
It was still touch and go.
And I knew the Reaper waited just outside,
The temperature still at fifty below.

Hour after hour the struggle went on
To save our baby's life.
Two frost-bitten fingers were lost from her hands,
Lost to the doctor's knife.

Under my breath I cursed the yellow metal,
The hateful thing called gold
That drew us from our home in the south
To live in the land of ice and cold.

There in the doctor's office
I finally bowed my head,
And, in despair, I asked the Lord to save her.
I still recall the words I said.

"Please save our baby,
And I'll leave this land of cold.
Return her to us,
And I'll forsake my search for gold."

Suddenly, as if that was what He was waiting for,
The fever broke. The danger was past.
The doctor said, barring complications,
Sara would live. She was gaining fast.

Out there on the edge of clearings,
A hooded figure turned to go
In search of one not so fortunate.
The pickings are good at fifty below.

Just one month later, to the day,
We left the land of cold,
Headed south to the warmth of the southern lands.
Let someone else muck for gold.

I'm sure the adventure's still there.
The great white bear still prowls in the snow.
But it's surf and sand for me and mine.
You can have your fifty below.

GREED

Now you ask me where I got my wealth.
Well, I guess I can tell you. I don't mind, for I'm growing old.
And it's important that you younger people understand
That greed can consume a man, and the consequences when you search
    for gold.

Now through the Valley of Serpents and along the Warrior's Path
Under the Hanging Coffins with daylight fading fast,
We knew we were close to the end of our quest. But we also knew that not
    far behind,
Others were on our trail, and a thirst for blood was on their mind.

For we were treading on sacred ground,
Desecrating even the dead in our mad rush for gold
Buried when our grandfathers were but children,
Stolen and hidden in days of old.

Could they but speak, the very rocks could tell us
Of blood spilled in this game of guns,
And point out the bleached bones of both good and bad,
Of battles lost and won.

On the branches of a giant cottonwood
Great dark birds sit and wait like grisly guardians.
They marvel at the stupidity of greedy men
And leave them to their fate.

Well, we cold camped that evening,
And we were up before the morning sun.
Each wrestled with the knowledge that
He'd be rich or dead before this day was done.

For we'd followed the map religiously.
No stone was left unturned.
We left but scant traces of our passing.
No bridge was left unburned.

Still our enemies trailed us like wolves.
They took the scent
And hung on to us like buzzards
No matter where we went.

FROM THE PEN OF BIG IRV LAMPMAN

There in the Valley of Skulls,
In the shadow of the cottonwood,
We found the spot marked on the map
And began to dig as fast as we could.

Ten feet down we struck a chest and,
In quick succession, a dozen more.
A king's ransom in gold and jewels, and
Yet, we were now greedier than we were before.

Now we looked at each other grudgingly and hands hung close to guns.
Time and greed were our biggest enemies now and suspicion.
For now we had each other to worry about,
And there were still many days of struggle ahead to get our treasure out.

High above us on the limbs of the cottonwood,
The great dark birds looked down. And I bet they grinned
And were making bets among themselves
That death would win again.

For the warriors of the forest waited back the way we came.
Up ahead, through swampland, our chances were about the same.
Ahead were gators and quicksand to hold a man and pull him down,
And sinkholes a man could step in and disappear without a sound.

But we weren't about to quit now. For if the cutthroats who had buried
 the chests
Had made it in here and out again,
We'd fight the swamp to our last breath,
And never, never give in.

Well, the warriors hit us at sunup,
At least seven hundred strong: a screaming horde,
Sweeping over us like an ocean wave,
And then, just like that, they were gone.

The air was filled with powder smoke.
Our ears half-deafened from the rifle's roar.
Then came the silence that seemed almost as deafening,
Leaving us five fewer than we were before.

▶

Mountain Yarns and Prairie Tales

We grabbed up the halters of the mules already loaded;
And, not even waiting to bury our fallen comrades in the swamp, we fled
    as fast as we could.
We could have traveled much faster leaving the gold behind,
But we didn't, even though we knew we should.

Lord, that swamp was an awful place,
The heat stirring, threatening to cut off our breath.
With moccasin snakes and gators waiting
For just one mistake, promising an awful death.

Our clothes stuck to us.
The insects threatening to drive a man mad.
Thirst an ever-present agony,
Trying to ration what little water we had.

Oh, there was water all right,
Sitting in stagnant pools
Not fit for man or beast.
The swamp's not a place to forget the rules.

At nightfall the mosquitos came:
Great buzzing clouds with their tiny needles, millions strong,
Their humming as they engulfed us
An incessant, maddening song.

Always we were urged to keep going
By a terrible, hopeless cry from someone who'd lagged behind.
The heat and suffering enough to make
Even the strongest lose his mind.

At last we staggered out of that hell hole,
Now only three.
The fever soon took the other two,
And now there's only me.

And the treasure? Well, most of it's there where we left it in the swamp.
Go get it if you want. I've got all I need.
But be mindful of the cost and remember the price paid
When men become possessed by greed.

FROM THE PEN OF BIG IRV LAMPMAN

I've got my home in the southern lands,
And I sit on my veranda and gaze out to sea.
With a pretty wife and children, I'm contented as a man can be.

Except sometimes in the night
When I smell again the powder smoke.
And in my nightmare I see a good friend killed
With a tomahawk—cut down with a single stroke.

All around our compound is the jungle,
Everywhere a verdant green.
Now I can never get enough fresh water,
Least so it seems.

And I'm constantly checking the screens on the windows,
Remembering when the mosquitos came to feed.
And I remember those who died out there
Still consumed by greed.

People wonder why I sometimes jump at the cry of a bird or a
    monkey's screech,
And I keep a gun primed and ready close to hand.
It's because sometimes the memories come crowding in, and
They're sometimes almost more than a man can stand.

But, I have my home, my servants keep my crop growing,
More than I'll ever need.
Was it worth it? I don't know.
It isn't easy to live with knowing you've sold your soul to greed.

THE HORROR AT OLD DRY WELLS

It's a land where the scorpion rules, but thirst is king, where the sun
    blisters and the rattler sings.
From this cauldron comes the tale I have to tell: the tale of the horror of
    Old Dry Wells.

Now there was a time when the water flowed fresh and cold
And gave life to young and old.
The wagons going West through this parched piece of hell
Could always count on water at the Old Dry Wells.
'Course they didn't call it that back then.
Both red and white came to drink, and it gave life to all kinds of men.
Some passed through, headed West to the gold fields to strike it rich,
    they said.
Some did; but more didn't, by gun or knife they'd wind up dead.

Some didn't even make it this far, leaving their bones upon the sand,
Victims of these stark and unforgiving lands.
In the cool of the evening, the wild things would come to slake
    their thirst;
And no one begrudged them, after all, they were here first.

But then something happened, and the wells went dry.
No one to this day can answer why.
Why, after untold years of being a life-giving force, the water slowed, then
    stopped, and the horror began?
Skeletons of man and beast began to dot this land.

Wagon trains heading West made it to the wells and died right there,
Adding their bones to those already there.
Men died and horses died. Oxen, too.
And as time went on, the legends grew
Of a place in the desert, a haunted place, where only thirsty horses dwell.
And so goes the story of Old Dry Wells.

I visited there, back in '69. I had the fever bad.
Lust for the yellow metal had claimed my soul and driven me mad.
I should have known something was wrong from the bones I started
    to see.
Man and beast, they seemed to rise up to beckon me.

FROM THE PEN OF BIG IRV LAMPMAN

"Come join us and help us with this story we have to tell.
Tell tales of the horror at Old Dry Wells."
It makes you wonder what it was that brought a curse upon this land.
Do the answers lie buried somewhere beneath these burning sands,
    just to give man a taste of hell through a place called Old
    Dry Wells?

Chapter 2

Ghost Stories

Hidden deep down in everyone is the fear of the unknown. Probably from when our ancestors huddled around a fire and cast fearful eyes into the darkness. 'Cause that's the nature of the beast.

THE LEGEND OF WILSON'S SLOUGH

Down in Louisiana in a sleepy little town,
People stay in their houses when the sun goes down.
They talk real quiet, and they drink a little brew.
Then the talk gets around to Wilson's Slough.

Now, everything that crawls and slithers hangs around that place.
The cypress hangs down to brush your face.
There's wildcats and gators in there, too.
There's something worse than that in Wilson's Slough.

Now, I had me a hound as mean as sin.
He'd fight anything. Every time he'd win.
If he'd a-tangled with the devil, I'd have bet on Blue.
He came a-whinin' for mercy out of Wilson's Slough.

Tail between his legs, belly scratching the ground,
He ain't so tough anymore when the sun goes down.
There's other good hounds been ruined there, too,
By whatever it is down in Wilson's Slough.

Oh, it's a hell of a place to be caught at night.
Even brave men will shake with fright.
Something comes a-crawling outta the ooze
And goes prowling down in Wilson's Slough.

A wino got lost and then went mad,
Driven out of his mind by the fright he'd had.
There's rattlesnakes and cottonmouths and copperheads, too,
All waiting to make your day down in Wilson's Slough.

You can lose all you got in a poker game.
After a while every drink gets to tasting the same.
If you're feeling real brave, wanna try something new?
Just spend the night alone down in Wilson's Slough.

Nobody's ever seen it 'cause it prowls at night,
'Cept that old wino driven mad with fright.
Maybe it's something left over from when the world was new,
And it feels right at home down in Wilson's Slough.

FROM THE PEN OF BIG IRV LAMPMAN

During the heat of the day, the heat holds you in its grip.
You can still feel the tension like the bite of a whip.
It gets its hottest long about two.
Nobody goes swimming in Wilson's Slough.

The night moves in like a funeral shroud,
Chorus of the night things a-singing loud.
Then the silence is there like a breath of dew
'Cause the thing's afoot in Wilson's Slough.

THE HOUSE ON HAUNTED HILL

Oh, yes, once its splendor
Was unsurpassed, belonging to
The people of a fine and prominent family
In a time now long gone past.

There were parties and dances
With lovely ladies in beautiful gowns,
Fielding the passes of young gentlemen
From the finest families in town.

The drapes were made of velvet.
Fine portraits graced the walls.
Chandeliers of finest crystals
Graced the long and splendid halls.

In those days there lived a girl there
Who dreamed of love and happiness, as young girls often will.
And so begins the story
Of the House on Haunted Hill.

Her family had always provided her
With the best of everything.
But she only wanted the boy she loved
To give her a wedding ring.

She didn't care if it was a diamond one,
A simple band would do.
A husband was what she longed for
And, someday, children, too.

But the boy that she had chosen
Was only a sailor by trade,
And her family despised him because
Of the little wages he was paid.

So they sent her off to boarding school,
And he went off to sea.
But before he left he carved a promise
In the garden on a tree.

From the Pen of Big Irv Lampman

Well, almost a year later the letter came
That her boy was lost at sea.
Her heart was inconsolable.
Her grief was terrible to see.

And so she pined away,
As the brokenhearted often will,
And some say she's up there
Mourning still.

She died on a cold and gray dawn
And was laid to rest on Haunted Hill.
They say sometimes you can hear her sobbing,
Sometimes when the night is soft and still.

Ruin came to the family. Their fortunes declined.
The rest of the children moved away.
A gloom seemed to settle over the place
Even on a sunny day.

The stories began then of a great white dog,
Her favorite, that mourned about her grave.
His sad eyes seeming to ask the question, "Why?"
As he stood guard above her grave.

But there's really nothing to be afraid of,
Only a sad and lonely shade mourning as the grief-stricken often will,
Mourning through the halls and gardens
Of the House on Haunted Hill.

THE NATURE OF THE BEAST

Out there in the darkness, when the doors are bolted for the night,
And out in the trees, just beyond the circle of warmth, revealed by the
    campfire light,
Something waits, something huge and dark and intangible. It watches with
    glittering eyes,
With an unholy hunger it watches every move and moves closer as the wind sighs.

We know from pierced and broken bones that, far back though the mists of time,
Primeval man crouching over his fire sensed it and cringed in fear
And heaped more fuel on the fire,
Terrified of the unknown, yet sensing it drawing near.

You can know it's there when the fire burns low and the shadows come
    creeping in.
Hurry now and build up the fire. No time to waste till the flames burn
    bright again.

Even in the city, with its myriads of artificial light,
It waits for society's unwanted back in the shadows where the light is not
    so bright.

What was that? Did you hear a twig snap out there beyond the circle of light?
Is that just a shadow at the edge of the trees? I don't know, better keep the fire
    burning bright.

For, you see, it's still hungry, just waiting to feast,
And no one is safe from its unholy hunger for that's the nature of the beast.

Shhhh....Listen. What was that? Whisper or sound?
Is it out there moving, or maybe it's just the wind moving the leaves around?

And when man goes home beyond locked doors in this world lighted by
    electric light,
I wonder if he's aware of two glistening eyes, waiting, staring from out there in
    the night.

I can just see lips curl back over glistening fangs and hear its rumbling growl
    waiting for the feast.
But, then it's patient. It always has been. For that's the nature of the beast.

IMAGINATIONS

Now you hear the sound of splashing water
Somewhere out in the night,
And a twig snaps from something stepping on it
Out of the circle of campfire light.
You tell yourself that there's nothing in the dark
That's not there in the daylight. But, then again,
You're ten years old and missing your mom.
Then the water splashes again.

You look at your best friend Tommy,
And he looks as scared as you.
They say that misery loves company, and
You've gotta admit it's true.
You listen to the sound of the night critters,
Crickets, frogs and things.
The frogs are croaking, an owl hoots,
The mosquitos brush you with their buzzing wings.

There's another sound that bothers you.
It aggravates you to no end.
It grates on your nerves, drives you nuts.
There's that twig snapping again.
The sound is your scoutmaster snoring.
Nothing bothers him.
Your eyelids are getting heavy, you do your best to remain on watch;
But it's a battle you just can't win.

All of a sudden, it's morning.
You've survived your first night in the woods.
You figure you're gonna tell them about those sounds you heard,
But you wonder if you should.
You try to tell yourself it was nothing;
But as the troop starts out, you hurriedly shoulder your pack,
For what you saw on the bank of the stream wasn't reassuring.
Imaginations don't leave tracks!

A BAD NIGHT ON SCARECROW HILL

When the chill winds of autumn rustle the leaves
And the night is cold and still,
As mortals sleep, the witches keep
Their Sabbath on Scarecrow Hill.

The scarecrows stand all in a row,
The wind makin' them dance insanely in the light of the moon.
Four frightened eyes glisten from the rows of corn,
Their owners back in the gloom.

The wind, blowing his hat aside,
Exposes a scarecrow's grin.
The wind catches his clothes and blows them askew
As the scarecrow dances again.

Something's awful funny to the Jack O' Lantern
Sitting up on a post, judging by his smile.
He sits there with his toothy grin,
Laughing all the while.

The witch hags dance all around in a ring.
They chortle and cackle in unholy glee.
The clouds move across the face of the moon—
It's a scene only the devil should see.

The watchers in the corn shake in fright.
Their lives depend on remaining still.
For it's the night of the witches' holiday—
A bad night on Scarecrow Hill.

There's two runaway boys shaking in fright
Who fervently wish they'd never left home,
Hiding there in the corn scared to death,
Willing their feet to take wings for home.

FROM THE PEN OF BIG IRV LAMPMAN

For, there in the night is a hellish sight,
On the night that's cold and still.
For, as sure as you're born, the devil walks here.
It's a bad night on Scarecrow Hill.

The firelight gives a hellish cast,
With its dancing reddish glare.
One figure with the face of a goat
Makes the watcher shiver in terror.

The chanting reaches a fever pitch.
Now there's an urge to kill.
God help the boys if they get caught.
It's a bad night on Scarecrow Hill.

At last, the boys can stand no more.
Fear lends wings to their feet. Of adventure, they've had their fill.
And, at last, they're awful glad to be home in bed,
Safe from a bad night on Scarecrow Hill.

THE COACH

The first time I remember, it was the night my grandmother passed away.
It had been dark and cloudy—a miserable, long, gloomy day.
Oh, we all knew she was going. The doctor said it was just a matter of time.
Dad gathered the kids, and lit the lamps. It was way past nine.

There was the usual crying and sadness. The family all gathered together
As if, with the strength of numbers, they could drive death away.
Dad said the prayer, asking the blessing,
As was the custom in that bygone day.

The next few minutes have haunted me over sixty years or more.
Never again would I be youthful and carefree as I'd been before.
Everyone else settled in for the night; but, for me, sleep wouldn't come.
It seems no matter how tired you are sometimes, you just can't sleep
    after a hard day's work is done.

Always I keep asking myself, was it some kind of hellish vision that I
    alone was meant to see?
Or was it some quirk of mind that was hidden deep in me?
For, as I sat there, enjoying the evening sounds,
Gently smoking my pipe, gazing down upon the twinkling lights of town,
I heard the rumbling of great wheels coming from the road,
The panting of struggling horses pulling a heavy load.

Then, as the coach pulled in sight, my hair stood straight on end.
And, even now, remembering, it's standing up again.
For, the horses that wore the harnesses were long ago bleached bones
That, for some ungodly reason, had taken on a hideous life of their own.

The coach that they were pulling was a huge and terrible thing
With ornate carvings of gargoyles and cherubs, all sitting around in a ring.
Around the railing at the top of the coach sat several great, dark birds,
    looking like witch hags sitting there.
They clacked their beaks and flapped their wings like demons in their lair.

FROM THE PEN OF BIG IRV LAMPMAN

A dark and cowled figure sat on the coachman's seat.
He handled the reins with leathery hands, a scroll with names upon it was
    in the brackets at his feet.
He wielded the whip over his terrible steeds
And shouted his commands, urging them on to greater and even
    greater speed.

A glow from somewhere inside the coach gave the windows a fiery glare,
And the eyes of the coachman glowed blood red, with an evil and
    terrible stare.
As it passed us, a wind breathed in its wake,
Like the cold of November winds blowing off the lake.

It stopped before our door, paused for a moment, then rolled on.
In the morning, as I had suspected, I was told Grandmother was gone.

And, though now that night was over sixty years ago,
I remember like yesterday the Death Coach. And there's one thing I know:
Every day I pick up the paper, there's another good friend gone.
I'm sure the coachman's still on the job. The Death Coach rolls along.

One of these days he'll come for me, and it'll be my turn to go.
Will the coach then pause at Heaven or Hell? I guess it's not for mortal
    man to know.
But, the one who sits upon the box and drives the coach, you can damn
    well bet he'll know.

STILL MR. PRESIDENT

Down shadowed halls, past shadowed walls,
Something moves at night.
Through the gloom, from room to room,
In sparse and flickering light.

When the tours are gone across the White House lawn,
A stately figure glides along his way.
The staff moves aside respectfully,
And the phantom seems to retire at the break of day.

Once, not long ago, a lost little girl told of a tall and gentle man
Who befriended her and helped her find her way.
And no one helping in the search
Will ever forget that day.

"Why was the big man crying, Mama?
Why was he so sad?
When I asked him if he'd ever been here before,
His eyes looked so sad.

"He said he'd been lost here, too,
A long, long time
In these halls and gloomy rooms.
And he said he missed the warmth of the sunshine."

Suddenly she cried, "There's the big man, Mama."
And she ran down the hall
And stopped beneath a picture
Hanging upon the wall.

To this day, I still feel the hairs at the back of my neck
Stand up and a chill go through me clear to the bone.
For it was Honest Abe in the picture,
Hanging there alone.

To the staff he's Mr. President,
A familiar figure in this place he once called home.
He stands gazing toward now silent battle fields.
All night long he paces alone.

FROM THE PEN OF BIG IRV LAMPMAN

Winston Churchill, England's greatest statesman,
The one who faced Hitler's might,
After spending one evening in the Lincoln Bedroom
Refused to spend another night.

He said he had awakened in the wee hours
To see a shadowy figure sitting gazing out the window.
"There can be no doubt as to what I saw:
It was Mr. Lincoln. I'd swear it in a court of law.

"He turned toward me,"
The great statesman would later say.
"He nodded slightly
And then just faded away."

Now it seems just recently
Another shade has joined Old Abe on his rounds.
They've been seen walking together
Under the trees out upon the grounds.

A much younger man, though just as dignified,
Stately and proud, he walks at night.
Just like Abe he retires
At the dawn's breaking light.

I wonder, does a love for our country
Forge a common bond?
Do they meet to discuss affairs of state
After the tourists are gone?

There's no doubt something moves at night
Across the grounds and through the gloom
Till the coming of morning light.

If you're startled by a breath, a chill,
Don't be frightened. It's just Mr. Lincoln going along his way.
If you're lucky you just might catch a glimpse,
Sometime 'round the break of day.

THE FACE ON THE STONE

Now, it's a quiet little resting place as such family graveyards often are.
The old folks pass on, the kids grow up and scatter near and far.
The grass and weeds take over. The stones weather away.
The wind at night whispers memories of those at rest here from long-
      forgotten days.

Our story comes to us from the bayou country,
Not really a place to harbor terror. Yet in the annals of evil it stands alone.
Such is the tale I'm about to tell you,
The tale of the face upon the stone.

The other graves have been deliberately placed to leave it
Off by itself, abandoned and alone.
When after years people came to right the stones
And cut the grass and weeds, it wasn't hard to see why
This particular grave stood off by itself so alone.

For when they turned it over, they gasped in fear,
For it was the face of Satan, carved upon the stone.
To the townspeople, it gave them cause to wonder and people say,
What kind of man lay there to have his stone carved that way?

Was it the family or the townspeople
Who marked the grave to let the man rest
Beneath the prince of darkness, and
Do the deeds he committed in life haunt his eternal rest?

But I know the answer, and it's a tale of foul murder
And of unspeakable acts better left unsaid.
For, if they be known to most of them as rest here,
It would even disturb the sleep of the dead.

The tale is about a man wealthy beyond imagining,
As the stories most often heard,
And of a brother living in the depths of poverty.
But of him never has there been spoken one bad word.

FROM THE PEN OF BIG IRV LAMPMAN

No, the man living in poverty was a good, decent man, so the stories go.
Oh, maybe sometimes given to restlessness, and maybe at times a little slow.
He did his best to eke out a living on his rocky and hilly little farm,
A man bent with hard work and struggle, a man of honest face and mighty arm.

He had but one joy in his drab and uneventful life.
As if in consolation, the Lord had seen fit to give him a beautiful, loving wife.
Beautiful she was, with golden hair shimmering like the sunbeams,
And a smile that would light the darkest room, least that's the way it seems.

It's said she loved her husband with a devotion
And tenderness unusual even in that bygone day.
Would that every man should be so lucky
To be loved and treasured that way.

Like everything else, the wealthy brother wanted her; and when the poor brother objected,
He was found murdered by unknown assailants, stabbed through the heart with a Bowie knife.
The rich man wanted it all. He desired his brother's wife.

When his advances to his brother's widow were turned away,
The rich brother vowed she would not be able
To speak of his foul deeds that could not stand the light of day.
So the widow had an accident, fell out of her bedroom window to the rocky path below.
How could such a thing happen wondered the townspeople? Only the night wind knows.

Only one complication: a girl child born in the marriage's second year,
Now in the early stages of adolescence, with adulthood drawing near.
Now the last piece of the puzzle, she suddenly disappeared.
Spirited off to a watery grave is what the townsfolk feared.

▶

Now, the rich man's house was a huge and evil thing,
Glowing like some obscure gargoyle over the town.
And not one shred of sunlight lingered there,
Not in the house or out upon the grounds.

As the years passed, stories began to surface of screams coming from the
    awful mansion
Terrible enough to send the townsfolk passing by, scurrying home
    in fright.

Years later, the rich man died and went to face his maker as every man
    must do.
He was buried far from the other graves and I have told to you.
Upon his grave no flowers grow, and upon his tombstone
Is the face of the prince of darkness. For his life he must atone,
So goes the tale of the murder most foul and the face upon the stone.

Just a few years ago, as the old mansion was being dismantled
To make way for a highway passing through,
The skeleton of a woman was found chained to a wall in the basement.
That's why her ghost walked, as ghosts often do.

I hope now that the monster is dead
And in Hell, paying for deeds for which he must atone.
The dead can finally find rest, and you can understand
The answer to the mystery of the face upon the stone.

*It has come to light that, about a year before his death, the
rich man was found wandering the halls of the mansion.
He'd been up all night; and, from that time until his death,
he remained undeniably quite mad.*

FROM THE PEN OF BIG IRV LAMPMAN

THE BELL WITCH

Now, on cold and windy nights, with the windows streaked with rain,
And the wind, passing on its way, rattles the window panes,
When unseen forces of this world shriek in unholy glee,
Then mortals shiver and shudder at the mention of Adams, Tennessee.

For ghostly appearances and frightful happenings in this quiet hamlet did abound.
And things dark and sinister happened at Adams town.
A mighty, marble monolith graces a final resting place,
And names are much respected and written on its face.

A young and innocent heart beat in the breast of Betsy Bell.
But, happiness for a long, long time avoided the queen of the haunted dell.
For, an unseen thing, an evil presence, destroyed a love that could have been,
And took the life of a good and honest man, out of the world of men.

The Bell Witch, that elfin wraith, danced upon the wind,
And stood at the bedside of old John Bell and grinned a death's head grin.
A potion concocted, a big dose given, and John Bell breathed his last.
And over the mourners was heard a ghastly song and an insane, chortling laugh.

Well, Bell Wood Park and a historical mark back up the legends they tell
Of an unseen fiend, a fearful thing, and the family known as Bell.
It's plain as day. There can be no doubt. It's there for all to see.
And, some say, the Thing's there yet, in Adams, Tennessee.

Now, what was this Thing? Was it spawned in the very foulest depths of Hell;
Or was it a form of judgment visited on the Bells;
Or did Satan, in an unguarded moment, leave open the door to Hell a crack,
And, then, have to send out his demons to drag the Thing, a-screamin', back?

NIGHTTIME ON THE MOORS

He stood before me, a pitiful thing,
His body tired and wasted and old.
His face burned brown by untold summer suns,
Then toughened by winter's cold.

But the eyes that burned into mine
Were clear, undimmed by the passing of time.
The pride that showed in that unbowed head
I hoped is reflected in mine.

Is it true, as I've been told,
You wish to spend the night on the moor?
Ah, 'tis a brave lad ye be,
For 'tis a fearful place and that's for sure.

I've seen the Hell Hounds, plain as day,
When the fog comes rollin' in,
And the witches dance around their fires
Each night when their celebration begins.

There's things that go floating through the night
That's got no business being there.
Why, I've even seen a brave soldier, lad,
Drop his weapon and run screaming in terror.

For when critters with wings wear a human face,
There's definitely something that's not quite right.
It's enough to make the bravest men
Take off in panicked flight.

The fog 'tis like nowhere else on earth.
It's cold and clammy and sticks to your skin
And penetrates clear down to your bones.
You swear you're in some unearthly place where no sun has ever shone.

FROM THE PEN OF BIG IRV LAMPMAN

The local folks lock up the livestock at night
For there's beasties that play on the moor.
And there's no guarantee even at that,
Even though they're behind locked doors.

For the blood lust is an all-powerful thing.
Only a bullet can end its sting.
You should know the howling out on the moor,
Laddy, it's a fearful thing.

But if you still want to go, well, come on then.
I'm as ready as I'll ever be.
You take the lead. I'll cover your back
'Cause it still scares the hell out of me.

THE MYSTERY OF O'FLAVERTY'S KEEP

There's gnarled burr oaks and half-dead pines
And water-carved stones from ancient times,
A brook that murmurs softly through the glens,
And there's a cry of sadness from the mourning winds.

No blade of grass grows on the lawn,
No voice of songbirds is raised in song,
For something, who knows what, has cursed this glen
And strikes without warning again and again.

The people who lived here withered away
And disappeared into some bygone day.
There's an old house frozen by winter's cold and baked in the summer heat,
So goes the mystery of O'Flaverty's Keep.

From time to time the town fathers
Planted grass and watched it turn to dust.
A beautiful wrought-iron gate, once a metal marvel,
Is now covered with rust.

No raindrops kiss these forsaken grounds,
And the constables shake their heads
As they pass on their rounds.
They ask themselves,
"When the rain all around the place falls in sheets,
Why not then on O'Flaverty's Keep?"

For you see, the horror of the place is that nothing lives.
It's as if the land, for whatever reason, no longer has life to give.
Across the street three green willows weep
As if in mourning for O'Flaverty's Keep.

You know, the thing man must ask himself is
What kind of malignant hatred haunts this glen?
What can suck the very life out of this land
Like some kind of hellish vampire that's alien to the world of men?

A few years ago, at the end of the last world war,
A plan was conceived to find a solution once and for all.

FROM THE PEN OF BIG IRV LAMPMAN

Surely, in this time of mechanized warfare and exploding technology,
    they'd soon know the answer.
But, again, the answer eluded them as they met the proverbial stone wall.

For no living organism existed
In the ground beneath their feet.
The curse held fast.
No life was there in O'Flaverty's Keep.

When a man wanders these grounds or
Roams through the house from room to room,
There's an overwhelming sense of foreboding,
Of depression and sadness, like heartbreak itself awaits there in the gloom.

No, folks, in all the annals of mystery,
This is a puzzle that just can't be beat—
The unbelievable questions of O'Flaverty's Keep.

But one man knows the answer,
And it haunts his every waking moment, and at night it disturbs his sleep.
He alone bears upon his soul
The nightmare of O'Flaverty's Keep.

He no longer smiles like he used to every day.
His shoulders sag with the weight of the secret as he goes along his way.

His hair is not thick as it used to be,
And it's turned from dark to white.
He's taken to jumping at shadows
Sometimes in the dark of night.

I marveled at the change in him the other day
When I met him on the street,
For he looked like the very wrath of God
Carrying alone the secret of O'Flaverty's Keep.

Only this morning the newspaper read
He had been found hanging dead.
The weight on his shoulders had become too heavy.
Now it's for him the willows weep;
And, somewhere on the grounds, something watches and waits.
And the curse goes on at O'Flaverty's Keep.

NIGHT HAUNTINGS AND REFLECTIONS

One night many years ago,
A night near the end of May,
I chanced to drift off into a peaceful sleep.
But, somehow, it didn't end up that way.

Was the Lord sending me a message?
I guess I'll never know.
But I'll never forget that eventful dream
From so many years ago.

Suddenly I found myself
There on Bunker Hill.
I ducked just in time as a musket ball whistled by,
Screaming loud and shrill.

Line after line of red-coated soldiers,
Like wheat before the thresher mower,
Some staggering and falling, others torn asunder,
Like chaff on the threshing floor.

Then everything again was darkness.
I drifted a while, it seemed.
When next I awakened, it was near
A town called New Orleans.

And, again, I heard the cannons thunder
And heard the rifles bicker and brawl.
And, again, came the scream of the wounded and dying.
And, again, I saw them fall.

From then on, an endless parade of battle after battle.
Each more terrible than the one before.
Then a million marching dead men, ghosts of our fallen dead,
Lost in our nation's wars.

From uniformed soldiers carrying long-barreled muskets,
To lynx-eyed men in buckskins marching by and saluting, then marching again.
Their uniforms and weapons were different,
But their faces all looked the same.

From the Pen of Big Irv Lampman

All hollow-eyed and fearful
Their eyes filled with pain,
And the banners of all the battles
Went slowly and endlessly past.

And I wrote them down and logged them reverently as they passed:
Shiloh, Bull Run, Gettysburg, San Juan and Pork Chop Hill, Iwo Jima,
Normandy, the Battle of the Alamo.
Gun fire from a thousand muskets set the sky aglow.

On and on it went
All through that awful night,
Each more frightening than the one before,
Leaving me shaking in fright.

'Til the blood-drenched soil
Could no longer hold the dead,
And the air seemed to be filled
With screaming balls of lead.

And then, suddenly, I awakened
And again I wondered why,
If man would ever learn his lesson,
How many more would need die?

Can't we stop and think before
Reaching for a gun?
Why not do the negotiating before
The killing's begun?

What a gift to give each other
And to those brave ones now asleep,
To be able to say we did our best
Before God's judgment seat.

And in Flanders Field now the poppies grow,
And in Arlington blazes an eternal flame.
Who was right and who was wrong?
To the dead it's all the same.

▶

And over a thousand battlefields,
When the sun goes down at night,
And the moon rises into the Heavens,
Bathing the world with its gentle light,

Do the ghost of warriors unnumbered
Mourn for lifetimes to soon gone?
And, marching to a different drum,
Do they sing their battle songs?

And, as for the ones they left behind,
Do their heartaches still go on?
Or have loved ones been reunited,
Which has been the Lord's plan all along?

FROM THE PEN OF BIG IRV LAMPMAN

BATTLEGROUND

It's a quiet and ghastly place, when only the night wind plays
Around the trees and over silent glens, remembering the bygone days
When the rifles snarled, the cannons roared, and the dead and the dying fell.
The air was thick with smoke, the ground shaking with shot and shell.
Now, there's only the gravestones, row upon countless row,
Stark and silent in the moonlight, reflecting the starlight's glow.

But, sometimes, they say, on an autumn night, when the frost fiends dance around,
You can hear the jangle of harnesses and whispered commands, voices muted to muffle the sounds.
And, once, I heard a click, a rifle's hammer raised from its resting place.
I remember the timid, "Halt, who goes there?" and the look of fear in a frightened face.

And, people say, when the moon's at its fullest, basking the battleground in its glow,
The ghost of a tall and bearded man appears as he did so long ago.
And, as he moves among the graves, he seems to halt now and then,
And say a prayer at this grave or that, as if saying hello to a fallen friend.

What was that? A passing ghost that passed with only a whisper of sound,
Or was it just the wind passing by, moving the leaves around?
The moon continues on its way as it has since time began.
What are our puny problems to it? How insignificant is man.

The gaunt and bearded man stands silently in the starlight's glow,
Shedding the tears again as he did over a hundred years ago.
My heart feels heavy in my breast, and I hurry to leave this place.
For, I can't stand it any longer—this awful sense of waste.
And on the autumn night, as the frost friends dance around,
Peace reigns, once again, over this battleground.

THE GARGOYLE

During the day it's not so threatening
Tho' it's still a gloomy place.
A gargoyle perches above the door,
A look of perplexity on his face.

But there's many silent hints
That something's not quite right,
And things will change dramatically
With the shadows of the coming night.

For the birds sing in every tree
Up and down the street.
No birds ever visit there,
Not even pigeons at the gargoyle's feet.

And, even in the steamy heat of summer,
There's suddenly a cold wind to chill the bones.
And you feel certain something's watching,
That you're never quite alone.

Have you ever felt a warning,
A prickling at the nape of your neck?
And, for no reason at all,
Suddenly you're a nervous wreck.

Out of the blue you're jumping at shadows.
Who knows, maybe it's true,
In all the vast grounds and buildings
Maybe there is something watching you?

Did a curtain move on the second floor,
A pair of cold eyes gazing down?
Is there something more threatening
In the gargoyle's perpetual frown?

FROM THE PEN OF BIG IRV LAMPMAN

And now it's early evening,
So far not a thing seems out of place.
Is there now a look of malevolence
Etched in the gargoyle's face?

Are the eyes that this afternoon seemed cold
And dead burning with a smoldering flame?
Are you fearful to look into them?
Are your legs now weak and lame?

And now suddenly all is darkness.
The insects cease their song.
The warning's now like a clanging bell.
Far from high above the door you can see something's wrong.

It makes you wish you had wings on your feet
To fly across this lawn.
Your heart catches in your throat.
By God, the gargoyle's gone.

For a moment you doubt your senses.
You know now it's true.
While you were watching him
The gargoyle was watching you.

And, you know, he's out there somewhere,
On his face a hideous grin.
And, you know, your life matters not a bit—
It's all a game to him.

For it'll do no good to pray.
No good to cry in fear.
For the one with the scythe,
He's the winner here.

CASSIE

Now Cassie lives down there in the swamp
Out where the black trees grow,
Where the pale moon shines and the night
Birds call and the cold swamp winds blow.
Her eyes lights up like coals of fire when
Hit by the lanterns glare.
I've been told by them that's seen 'em
They're like a hungry gator's stare.

Now, they lived down at the edge of the swamp
In a run down shotgun shack.
There was pa and ma and three half-grown kids
And a pack of hounds they kept in the back.
The oldest sister grew up and moved away,
Leavin' Cassie to roam the swamps alone.
I guess she preferred it out there with the critters
Rather than what was waitin' for her at home.

They say that old man was kin to the Devil
And the old lady stirred a witch's brew.
By and by, as time went on, you could see
That boy turnin' devil, too.
But it was that girl that drove men
With a come-on you couldn't miss:
Face of an angel and the soul of somethin' else,
Cruel and cold as a cobra's kiss.

Word has it she found her sweetheart, one night, with her sister.
After that Cassie was twisted inside.
No man ever got near her again
Tho' there was no end to them that tried.
Then they found that no-good, floatin' in the water.
A gator had bit him clear in half.
And, as they pulled what was left of him out of the water,
They heard a woman's insane, cackling laugh.

FROM THE PEN OF BIG IRV LAMPMAN

Now the old man and the boy got caught
Stealin' horses, and they strung 'em to a cypress tree.
The old lady drowned in the swamp.
Cassie got away free.
Now, the swamp's an eerie, primeval place,
Out where the sawgrass waves.
It will hide you, caress you, and take you
To an early grave.

Well, Cassie is out there somewhere with her critters
And her mojo bones.
Be I you, I'd stay out'n that place and leave Cassie
And her critters alone.
'Cause out there somewhere, my friend,
The Devil walks. The locals all agree.
And they avoid the place after dark, like the plague,
'Cause old Cassie still roams free.

THE ANNIVERSARY

Now, I was traveling through the Midwest and right afer dark one night,
It came up a storm like I had never seen.
The wipers were goin' full speed, slip-sloppin' across the windshield
And my eyes were about to fall out tryin' to see through the wind and rain.

It was the darkest night I'd ever been caught in and about all I could do
Was slow my old truck down and try to follow the white lines.
And, sure enough, like it always does, trouble comes in bunches,
Like Dad used to say. And there it was, a detour sign.

Well, I managed to get pulled off onto this two lane
And fervently hoped I'd find somewhere to spend the night.
But I'd about given up hope and was lookin' for some place to pull off
When up ahead I saw some lights.

And, what do you know, a big truck stop
And a more welcome sight I never hope to see.
With fuel islands and showers
And a hot cup of coffee just waitin' for me.

There's nothin' like truck stop coffee
To take the chill off the bones.
I was the only customer that time of night
So I sat down to my coffee alone.

The waitress was a tiny blonde.
"You sure are a pretty little thing," I said,
As she came over to give me a refill.
And she just smiled in a sad kinda way.
Something about her kinda touched me,
So I left her a dollar when I got up to pay.

Well, I went on out to my sleeper, figurin' to catch a few winks.
No sense pullin' out with the storm goin' on that way.
And I must have slept like a baby
'Cause when I woke up, it was close to breakin' day.

FROM THE PEN OF BIG IRV LAMPMAN

Well, I crawled out, figurin' I'd have some more of that coffee.
But, for pity sake mister, there was nothin' there.
No truck stop anyway, just a couple of burned-out buildings.
And, I was, huh, I had no idea where.

Well, I got the old truck turned around
And headed back the way I had come last night through the rain.
I figured it was the best chance to find fuel;
And, as I drove, I wracked my brain.

Had I driven on in my sleep sometime during the night,
Only to awaken at dawn's early light?
Had I imagined that truck stop,
So welcomed there in the night?

No, I felt in my pocket and there was a book of matches
With the restaurant's label, plain as day.
It sure beats me, mister.
I don't know what else to say.

Well, I followed the detour and found a fuel depot;
And while I was fillin' up, I asked this old fella playin' pump jockey
About the place I'd spent the night.
Well, boys, that old fella's eyes just filled up with tears,
And he turned a ghastly white.

"Son, I used to own that place you're describin'.
But somethin' sure ain't right.
Because there's no way
You could have had coffee there last night.

"You see, that waitress you're describin',
Well, she was my daughter. But she died when we had the fire.
Ask any of the drivers, they all know.
I lost her on exactly last night, over twenty years ago."

VANISHING OLIVER LARCH

Christmas Eve, many years ago,
Fresh snow upon the ground,
Merriment and happiness,
Good friends gathered 'round.
The cheery glow from the fireplace
Gave off warmth to warm the heart.
So began our tale of mystery
Of vanishing Oliver Larch.

The old beloved carols were sung.
A great time was being had by all,
Mistletoe in the hallway,
A tree in the corner standing straight and tall.
Then the water bucket was found to be empty,
So goes the story they continue to tell.
His father asked Oliver to put on his jacket
To fill it from the well.

Picking up the bucket, Oliver started out the door.
Just a moment later his friends were startled by Oliver's screams of horror.
"Help! Help! They've got me!"
And as his father rushed out in the snow,
The bucket was found twenty feet to the right.
No tracks in the new fallen snow.

Their frantic calls were filled with fear
For the boy they love.
His terrified screams were growing fainter
Coming from above.
And, finally, they faded completely,
And no answer has been found to this day.
No plausible theory is there
To how he disappeared that way.

It was before the days of planes.
No bird could lift a boy of Oliver's weight.
No balloon was aloft that night.
So what carried Oliver to his fate?
The bucket was found twenty feet to the right.
No footprints made their mark.
So the questions remain. What happened to vanishing Oliver Larch?

FROM THE PEN OF BIG IRV LAMPMAN

THE LIGHT ON CHAPEL HILL

Sometimes in the evening
When the night is soft and still,
The people come from miles around
To gather at Chapel Hill.
They come by car and horseback,
By flash and lantern light,
They all come to glimpse the mystery
As it goes floating through the night.

They come with sandwiches and potato salad
And coffee by the mug,
With blankets and folding chairs
With beer and whiskey jugs.
The children play hide and seek,
Lovers hold hands and court by lantern light.
From motorcycles to hotrods
All gather in the coming night.

The kids play with sparklers
That brighten up the gloom.
But all festivities are off at darkness.
The fun's over way too soon.
For come the twilight,
Everything becomes quiet and still.
For the reason everyone is here
Is the light on Chapel Hill.

Many have tried to explain it
As a passing auto's lights.
But when no cars are allowed,
It still comes floating through the night.
It's been photographed and documented,
And the mystery's remaining still.
And still they come by hundreds
To see the light on Chapel Hill.

Now, there was a brakeman killed
On a railroad many years ago.
Could it be the brakeman's lantern
Giving off that eerie glow?

▶

Sometimes it moves from side to side.
Other times, up and down; and sometimes remains quite still.
Old men scratch their heads and mumble
About the light on Chapel Hill.

Well, as for me, I'll be content
To remember the night I spent that was peaceful and still
With good friends by a campfire
Viewing the light on Chapel Hill.

Maybe someone in a future time
May find an answer to Chapel Hill.
I choose to hope, my friends,
That no one ever will.
For man needs his mysteries
To whisper about on winter nights
To entertain young and old
With tales of the Chapel Hill.

FROM THE PEN OF BIG IRV LAMPMAN

THE RIDER OF PHANTOM HILL

Now, as something flits by on gossamer wings,
And the crickets and katydids and the night bird sing,
As ethereal phantoms dance across the dew-laden grass,
And you feel a shadow as something glides past,

The fog moves in to caress your face.
Was it in regret to shroud this place?
What is it you can feel in the air that brings a chill?
What happened here on Phantom Hill?

For there are legends about this place that all's not as it seems,
Although it's peaceful and quiet and lush and green.
There's a gloom that seems to pervade the air and add to the chill.
So goes the tale of Phantom Hill.

There's an old church that stands guard at the top of the hill
And, at the edge of the river, an abandoned mill.
It's just such a place where legends play
In the cool of the night, 'til break of day.

And, on warm summer nights as the moon shines down
And the night things sing their song,
Long about midnight when most are asleep
A rider comes loping along.

The horse he's riding is a mighty Morgan.
It makes not a sound as they pass by.
And the moon up there just takes one look,
Then speeds its passage across the sky.

He looks neither to the left or right
As he goes his lonely way.
And he speaks not a word as he continues his ride
Till the sky is streaked with grey.

He reins in a moment and gazes as if, in sad reflection,
At the ruins of an abandoned mill.
And you can sense a terrible sadness
In the rider of Phantom Hill.

▶

Who is there to take note of this ride
On this night that's so quiet and still?
Maybe only the bats that have taken up residency
In the cave on Phantom Hill.

Or maybe the great, grey wolf, home from his nocturnal prowling
To his den at the base of the hill.
He raises his voice in sympathetic communion
With the rider of Phantom Hill.

The waning moon now bids goodnight
As it gives way to the coming day.
And the slumping figure on the great war horse
Returns on his lonely way.

Here and there a bird awakens and twitters
In sleepy disarray.
And somewhere a rooster raises his voice
To announce the coming day.

And come tonight, it'll begin again
At the call of the whippoorwill.
All nature will hush for a moment
To welcome the rider of Phantom Hill.

It makes you wonder what long-ago
Tragedy could have happened at the abandoned mill.
What terrible secrets disturbs the rest
Of the rider of Phantom Hill?

Will he ever find peace? Who knows,
But I'm afraid he never will.
For he's been riding here for over a hundred years,
This lonely rider of Phantom Hill.

FROM THE PEN OF BIG IRV LAMPMAN

PUMPKIN HOLLOW

There's a place where I won't lead and I sure won't follow after dark.
I've no wish to be there on the road through Pumpkin Hollow.
It's a place that the moon tries to avoid. It's cold and spooky and dark,
Where the crack of a twig will take your breath away.
And cold, clammy hands clutch at your heart.
Where scary things turn out to be just what you were afraid they were.
They make your breath catch in your throat, making it hard to swallow.
'Cause an old stump can turn out to be something else
When you're on the road through Pumpkin Hollow.
Things with wings flit by in the night; and shiny, green eyes pierce the gloom.
You might try to act "macho," but it's a sham. Your courage wavers way
    too soon.
There're jack-o-lanterns with toothy grins. Frost jewels glitter in the grass.
An owl glides by on silent wings, trumpeting his haunting cry as he flies past.
What's that shadow behind the tree? You hurry by, hoping it won't follow.
But you look over your shoulder and there it is. You're on the road though
    Pumpkin Hollow.
A scarecrow stands his lonely vigil over the cornfield upon the hill.
The waning moon nods as it passes by every night, as it's done for untold
    years—and always will.
A great, dark bird looks down from its perch, and croaks out his ghastly
    cry—you can bet he's no swallow!
He a king vulture, ruler of all he surveys, down on the road through
    Pumpkin Hollow.
A cold fog moves through the trees and surrounds them like a shroud.
The moon's hidden just for a minute by the passing of a lonely cloud.

Chapter 3

Stories of the Sea

There is an area on Earth that the least is known about and yet it is well known as the most haunted place on Earth. That's the world's oceans. No other place holds more adventure and yet more terror.

THE DEVIL FISH

He was as hard as nails, a cranky old cuss,
With a face as hard as chiseled stone,
A face that had faced a thousand gales
Where the wind had cut clear to the bone.

The blue eyes that lit that face were
As clear as they'd ever been.
And he gripped my hand with a grip of steel,
Hard as the rest of him.

"So, you've come to hear about the Devil Fish.
Well, matey, I'm here to tell you it's true.
And, if ye'd be so kind as to buy me a drink,
I'd be proud to tell this tale to you."

Well, I signaled the innkeeper and told him to
Leave the bottle, and the old fella downed a dram.
Then he leaned back in his chair,
Thought for a moment, and then he began.

"'Twas but a few years ago, and I'd signed on
To a fishing vessel; and things had been going well.
We'd filled our hold and were about to
Head in, when we caught something straight from Hell.

"The first any of us knew, the net caught on something,
And there it stopped us dead.
It was caught on a reef, was the general belief.
'Reel it in,' the captain said.

"Well, the winch started to pull in the net,
And then began to smoke and then to groan,
Then stopped cold, still like, under the weight
Of a ten-ton milling stone.

"And, then, the line went slack.
Something was coming up out of the deep.
And, as we saw its shape while still deep in the water,
It looked like a huge, ugly spider; and my flesh began to creep.

"But it was the size of the thing that was beyond belief!

FROM THE PEN OF BIG IRV LAMPMAN

"The body was as big as the ship, and each arm,
Reaching out for a hundred yards or more,
And in the middle of the head, a great hooked beak
And two cold eyes to hold us fast with horror."

Here the old man paused a moment.
His face turned white, and he downed another dram.
His eyes seemed to look backward into something
Too terrible to remember. Then, once more, he began.

"The arms were now slithering on deck searching,
Hunting to catch a man and hold him fast and pull him down.
The arm would catch on something and then release
And move on with a sucking sound.

"The first to go was the cabin boy, pulled from the top
Of the mainsail where he held on at the very peak,
Caught by one of those awful arms to be pulled into the sea
To be bitten in two by that terrible beak.

"And, tho' his voice is now silenced forever,
Sometimes in the night I awake
And hear that scream and see again
Those pitiless eyes haunting my dreams.

"The ship was now listing. I swear the thing
Was trying to climb on board. We broke out the rifles
And began to fire, 'cept the fella we called the parson
Was on his knees asking help from the Lord.

"Now, young fella, I've heard it said that a ship
Will cry out when it goes to its death.
Well, I'm here to tell you I've heard that sound
When the Devil Fish held us fast and was
Beginning to pull us down.

"Then the cook came running with a kettle of boiling water
And threw it straight into one of those eyes.
And the thing roared in pain and hate
And squirted ink as dark as the midnight sky.

▶

"Son, I want to tell you I've seen hate before,
  But nothing like what I saw in those obsidian eyes as black as sin.
  And, then, just like that, the beastie let go and was gone,
  Just a ripple or two was all that was left
  To tell us the Lord had answered our prayers, and thank God it was gone.

"Along with it, four of our shipmates
  Taken by a terrible death; and, as the
  Parson raised his hands in thanksgiving, we did, too,
  Cursing the thing under our breath.

"And, you know, matey, the unsettling thing is
  Where there's one, there's two;
  And where there's two,
  You can bet there are a few.

"Out there in the sea somewhere swims a thing
  Of which nightmares are made.
  And, as the years go by, all I can hope for
  Is that my memories will begin to fade.

"And, maybe the time will come when my sleep
  Won't be haunted by the screams of the cabin boy
  From out of the past, plucked like an apple,
  By that terrible thing from the top of the mast.

"Well, my boy, that's the story of the Devil Fish.
  And, for what it's worth, I'll swear it's true.
  And for the bottle and the lend of your ears,
  My thanks go out to you."

Here ends my story about an old sailor
That had seen something out of the depths of hell.
And a story he, by luck or something more, lived to tell.
Anyway, it makes for darn good listening.
So, enjoy it—the tale of the Devil Fish.

FROM THE PEN OF BIG IRV LAMPMAN

THE MYSTERY OF THE *MARY CELESTE*

Now, the sea is full of mystery
From the Atlantic in the east
To the mighty Pacific in the west.
Nowhere in the annals of seafaring can you find such a tale as this:
The tale of the *Mary Celeste*.

I want to make sure I've got this right before I tell this tale to you.
She was abandoned and adrift in 1872.
She was watertight and seaworthy,
Missing her lifeboat and her crew.
Provisions were there, coffee on the stove,
And the gear of the captain and crew.

No signs of violence could be seen.
No bloodstain or weapons here.
The more they looked, the mystery deepened.
There began the first touches of fear.

A partially written letter abandoned in haste
Was absolutely the only clue.
No trace was there, save that
Of the *Mary's* captain and crew.

Could it have been pirates
That put the brave crew to the test?
Or did something much more sinister
Happen to the *Mary Celeste?*

Some unexplained and terrible sickness perhaps...
But, why abandon ship?
Why leave a sound and sailable craft
To be foolishly cast adrift?

The table was set for the evening meal.
The coffee pot still warm.
Who in his right mind would leave his ship?
No sailor ever born.

After a hundred years the questions are remaining still.
But whenever men sail the sea, they still wonder and, no doubt, always will.
But people will always wonder and never abandon their quest,
Somehow, somewhere, to find an answer to the mystery of the *Mary Celeste.*

SOMETHING DRAWING NEAR

This is a tale told to me by an old sailor who swore this story was true.
I made up my mind to believe him. Whether you do, my friend, is up to you.

Sometimes at night the fog comes rolling in.
Not quite a rain, it hides the sea
And chills the bones,
Then goes rolling out again.

It's spooky out here in the fog.
A man could imagine almost anything,
What with the whisper of sails
And hearing the ship's bell ring.

'Twas on just such a night as this:
The fog as thick as soup,
The crew on deck trying to see through the mist,
All standing around in a group.

The cook had brought us coffee
To try to ward off the chill.
A cold at sea can just as easily
Turn into a fever and kill.

The fog horn every now and then
Would reach out across the sea.
And I thought how like the call of some primeval beast,
Least that's the way it sounded to me.

The captain had just come out on deck,
I guess to reassure the men.
He nodded to me as he passed by,
Then the fog horn sounded again.

And it was answered.
But no fog horn ever made a sound like that—
A plaintive cry coming across the reaches of time—
Made my hair stand up to pierce my hat.

Somewhere out there across the water
Something heard our call.
And a light from atop the bridge turned to try to pierce the fog,
Now almost as solid as a wall.

From the Pen of Big Irv Lampman

Then that call out there in the night
Came to us again, nearer now,
And the sound of splashing water
Somewhere off the bow.

Then waves began to rock the ship,
And a smell of mold
And the awful smell of rotting fish
Left to spoil too long in the hold.

And the fool blowing the horn
Blew the damn thing again.
And the answering cry was almost on top of us,
Almost panicking the men.

Off the stern we could hear
The sound of splashing; and, at the same time, off the bow,
The wake of whatever it was
Threatening to swamp us now.

Then, just as suddenly, a tremendous disturbance
In the wake, like something turning around and swimming away.
And an almost plaintive cry of disappointment,
You could hear it plain as day.

Once or twice more we heard it,
And then that was all.
And, after twenty years at sea,
I never again heard that call.

We slept precious little that night
And for many a night to come.
And still the questions remain,
After my years at sea are done.

What was it out there in the fog?
I guess we'll never know.
But not a man will ever forget that sound
Heard so long ago.

THE MAELSTROM

He looked, for all the world, like a grizzly
As he stood alone at the bar,
His hands showing the signs of years of work,
Gnarled—marked with scars.

He lifted his glass and stared at us
With ill-disguised disdain.
His face was old and lined,
Aged by the wind and rain.

"So ye think ye be old
Sea dogs now ready to face the sea.
Well, after I've told this fine tale to you,
Let's see how ready you be.

"Once off the coast of the Northern Lands,
Not far from Hudson's Bay,
The sea suddenly turned dark as night
Where had been a fair and sunny day.

"And she began to whirl under our decks,
Tryin' to pull us down.
And rocks seemed to rise out of the depths,
The wind doing its best to run us aground.

"Then out of the sky came a waterspout,
Its width two miles or more.
They're a hundred times worse, you know, at sea
Than they've ever been ashore.

"Then a sound began, a mighty rumble,
The likes of which I hope I'll never hear again,
And, believe it or not,
Almost drowned out by the shrieking of the wind.

"A great sucking and gurgling sound
Like water going down a drain,
And you almost strangled to death,
Facing the wind and rain.

"Then up ahead at last we saw it,
Like the gaping maw of Hell,

From the Pen of Big Irv Lampman

And there was a ship caught in its clutches
Like a lost soul at the gates of Hell.

"The Maelstrom— all my life I'd heard of it.
And there it was as plain as day.
And I knew I was being drawn to the jaws of death,
Figured I'd die that very day.

"For there was a mighty man of war
Tossed like a cork upon the wave.
Then down she went with all hands,
Headed for her watery grave.

"And I saw a mighty whale,
Eighty feet or more long,
Tossed in the air like a flounder—
In another second, gone.

"Aye, mateys, I screamed with the rest,
Fear driving us almost insane.
I admit it now, straight to your face.
Any sailor will tell you the same.

"Then something fetched me hard on the head,
And the darkness came closing in.
The stars were out and the moon just risen
Before I opened my eyes again.

"I lay on my belly on a tiny island,
The only one left to tell the tale
Of the day at sea when Hell opened up
And I swore I would not fail

"To thank the Lord every day of my life
That I was chosen to live.
For whatever reason I'll never know,
Life was His to take or give.

"So, if you're still determined to sail the seas,
Boys, brave you need be.
For I've been to the abyss and returned,
And once is enough for me."

THE VOICE

He sat in his rocking chair,
An old warrior whose battles were over long ago.
He sucked on his pipe
To set the ember aglow.

I'd heard he had a story to tell
That was different from the rest.
And it was hard to curb my impatience
Tho' I did my best.

He seemed to be lost somewhere
In years long gone by.
He seemed focused on something far away,
Gazing into the sky.

Then he began to speak in a voice
Only slightly weakened by his years.
And he straightened in his chair
As he pulled the veil back away from the years.

'Twas toward the end of the big war
On one of Her Majesty's fleet.
And many a ship was with Davy Jones,
Lost in the clutches of the deep.

And I had just taken the watch.
It was a cold and foggy night.
And I prayed long and hard to make it
Through till the morning light.

My ears strained against the fog
For even a whisper of the Kaiser's screws,
My hand on the rope to give warnings
To the captain and the crew.

For these were dangerous waters
Where the Kaiser's wolf packs were known to prowl.
And no mistake was allowed on watch,
Fair weather or foul.

FROM THE PEN OF BIG IRV LAMPMAN

When, suddenly, over the railing came something straight out of hell
That caused my breath to catch in my throat.
And a cold, more chilling than any nor'easter,
Penetrated through my coat.

For, what had once been a man
Climbed over the rail and stood upon the deck.
A patch covered one of his eyes.
He wore the colors of some forgotten wreck.

A cutlass was thrust through his belt,
A dagger between his teeth.
A scar from a knife marked his chin,
A puckered hole from a bullet marked his chest underneath.

Dark and horrible stains covered his shirt.
His one good eye fixed me with a cold and terrible glare.
And I felt my heart begin to fail me
From the awfulness of that stare.

Then he said with a rasp, "Stand fast, matey.
You've naught to fear from me.
For I'm only a wandering soul
Lost upon the sea."

He moaned and wailed and rattled the chains
That were clamped about his feet,
And scared the hell out of this sailor
Of Her Majesty's fleet.

"I came to right a wrong
From so many years ago.
Lives taken must be replaced,"
He cried, pacing to and fro.

"We sent a ship to the bottom
For no other reason than greed.
Three hundred souls lost, murdered;
And, to me, there was no need.

"And for three hundred years I've prayed for forgiveness,
Never knowing rest.
And now I've come to ask your help
To aid me in my quest."

"Dreadful apparition,
What do you want of me?
Only He who rules the universe
Alone can set you free."

And he shrieked and moaned and rattled his chains
And told me to change our course hard right. He ordered me,
And he drove his dagger into the rail
When I told him I couldn't agree.

"Turn aside. Turn aside
Or join me with Davy Jones.
There is but a moment to decide.
The decision is yours alone."

"Terrible apparition,
Please tell this sailing man
Why must we change direction?
Why put it in my hands?"

And then I heard a voice,
A kind and gentle one,
That ordered me to change the course
To avoid the Kaiser's guns.

"As for you, my child, don't you know
The moment you asked forgiveness, it was given thee.
Only the repentance in your heart
Is what set you free.

"All these years, never knowing peace,
You've let your burdens grow.
The chains you wear you forged yourself with guilt,
For I forgave you long ago."

FROM THE PEN OF BIG IRV LAMPMAN

"Hard right," I cried
And rang the warning bell.
How close we came to disaster
I could never tell.

But the torpedoes went on by.
Our change of course had saved the day.
Tho' I was decorated for my decision,
Why I made it I could never say.

But in my room
I have something to back up my tale—
For he forgot to take it with him—
The dagger in the rail.

And now my years are winding down.
Soon I'll rest beneath the sod.
But I fear it not a bit
For once I heard the voice of God.

SKELETON ISLAND

'Twas on the tenth of April
When we spotted that tiny strip of land
And doubted there would be anything
Of interest on that miserable stretch of sand.
For only the sparsest of vegetation
Was apparent as we drew near
And the sound of breakers was all we could hear.

As it was late in the evening, the captain decided to wait
Until morning before going ashore to investigate.
And it was decided to send a crew of five worthies, fully armed,
For these were dangerous waters, make no mistake.

For those were the days of sailing ships,
And both privateers and pirates plied their trade.
But, also, a time of strong men and opportunity,
Of fortunes lost and made.

Well, the next morning as we set foot upon the shore,
We were no more impressed than we had been before.
For nowhere could we find a sign of life,
And something, I couldn't tell yet what,
Cut the air with tension like the sharpest knife.

We spread out to search for fruit or fresh water,
But nothing of the like could be found.
And over all the oppressive silence, the breakers the only sound.
Then I heard one of the men yell, his voice high with terror.
The panic in his voice brought a tingling to my hair.
When I reached his side and saw where he was pointing,
Suddenly my heart was in my throat.
And I fervently wished I was off this God-forsaken beach and back aboard
    the boat.

For in a makeshift shelter was the skeleton of a man sitting gazing out to sea,
As if watching, waiting for who knew how long, and only water as far as the
    eye could see.
Lying beside the chair was an empty bottle of rum,
I guess to give some relief from the loneliness and the unrelenting sun.

FROM THE PEN OF BIG IRV LAMPMAN

A few weathered pages were in a bound journal in his lap,
Empty eye sockets gaped from the time-yellowed skull beneath his hat.
I picked up the journal. I figured he wouldn't care,
And, as I read the story, unfolded his last days of terror.

"Water all gone now; at least, water I can drink.
There's a little more rum, but no food
Since we hit the reef that caused our ship to sink.
And for the past few days now, I've felt the cold hand of Death
    upon my shoulder.
But I no longer fear Him. I guess I view Him as a friend now, tho' I'm not
    growing bolder.
But before I join my shipmates in the hereafter, wherever seamen go,
I wish to set the record straight. But if it will ever be read, God only knows.
Now, I've been on many a good ship and some not so good.
And generally I've been no better or worse
Than any man, tho' there's a few things I would change if I could.
For, I've been a hard-drinking man at times and known
Many a woman tho' I've never married a one.
Spent most all I ever made, I did, on the ladies and many a cask of rum.
But there was one time I'm ashamed of, a foul murder committed on a deck.
A captain, his wife and child sent to Davy Jones, robbed them, they did,
    and set adrift the wreck.
Oh, I took no part in it myself, but I kept silent when a man should tell.
And very soon now I'll carry the guilt of it with me straight to Hell.
Oh, what I wouldn't give for a wee sip of fresh water to cool my tongue.
It seems even the air is afire. As I draw it in, it seems to burn my lungs.
At night the ghosts of men I left dead come to bedevil me
With gaping eyes and silent screams, they come walking out of the sea
With seaweed caught in their hair and, over all, the stench of death.
And I scream and scream till I can scream no more, I have to stop and
    catch my breath.
And they point at me reproachfully as I cringe and cry.
And as they gaze at me they ask the question, 'Why?'
Why must a cutlass or pistol always be close to hand?
How can I answer that, dying as I am, on this miserable strip of sand?
Well, the rum's almost gone now, and not a sail can I see.

▶

I hope if someone finds me, he'll leave me here watching,
For that's where my heart is, out there on the sea.
And, if I'm to haunt this world, let it be on a ship
To hear again the sound of the wind in the rigging and watch Saint Elmo's
    Fire along the sails,
And hear the crack of thunder and the sizzle of lightning and, upon the deck,
    the patter of hail.
No, I'd never be happy, even in the next world, without a deck on which
    to stand.
For, you see, it gets in your blood, and it's your lot forever once you're a
    seafaring man.
Well, the light seems to be fading. I regret only that I have no more
Rum to drink a toast to you, the one who finds me.
And if you're a likely lad, you'll leave me as you found me.
It's not the worst thing to have your own island.
I trust that you'll agree, and, maybe..."

And there it ended, and I carefully closed his journal and placed it in his cap.
And I almost wish I could have known him in his long forgotten-day.
The next morning we set sail and sailed away,
And left him sitting there on Skeleton Island.
We honored his wishes as, I hope, will the next who finds him in
    some future day.

FROM THE PEN OF BIG IRV LAMPMAN

THE DUTCHMAN

Now, wherever men gather to spin their tales of the sea,
And, whenever men go down to the sea in ships, on one thing they all agree:
There's many a thing that's happened out there that's beyond the scope of man,
And many things happen far at sea that they don't understand.

For there's those that swear they've seen shipmates walking on the waves,
Who long ago sank into the deep, down to their watery graves.
There's those who have seen the mermaid and heard her siren song,
And watched as she beckoned and dreamed of her once she'd gone.

As for me, yes, I've a tale to tell. And, yes, I'll swear it's true.
Though I'm sure you'll say I'm mad after I've told this tale to you.
But, to me, that makes no difference. My sea faring-days are past.
The days that I'll grace this mortal coil are speeding by so fast.

Once, many years ago, rounding the Cape under sail
On one of those rare moonlit nights as I watched a passing school of whales,
Faraway across the water, I saw an approaching sail.
Her deck seemed deserted, and she gave no answer to my hail.

Not a light shone upon her deck, and there was not a whisper of sound.
I could see no one on watch though rocks and reefs abound.
Suddenly, a wail of terror seemed to cause my blood to freeze
And become as ice in my veins and brought a tremble to my knees.

'Twas the ship's dog that had come to stand at my feet,
And he let out another wail of terror like a lost soul at the judgment seat.
His hair stood straight on end, his tail between his legs,
As he cowered there behind me behind some water kegs.

Then, as she passed us, at last I saw the name
That had inspired fear in the hearts of men and stained the sea with shame.
For, it was the *Dutchman*, and she was such a fearful sight
That sometimes still I awake in a cold sweat of terror, sometimes in the night.

Wherever men gather to spin their tales of the sea,
They've got one eyewitness, boys—*me*.
If you say I'm mad, that matters not to me
For I've seen one thing in this world, my friend, that simply cannot be.

▶

What I saw on that deck as the *Dutchman* sailed on past
Will haunt my every nightmare, though I spent twenty years before
    the mast.
Standing at her helm was a man, long since dead,
With a terrible death's head grin to fill my soul with dread.

Every time she rolled, he seemed to beckon with bony hand,
Eyes afire with the flame of madness as he searched in vain for land.
I know as well as I know my name
That he's still out there somewhere, still paying the price of shame,
Still he faces into the gale and hurls curses into the wind,
Doomed to sail on forever, a stranger to the world of men.

FROM THE PEN OF BIG IRV LAMPMAN

HELL SHIP

'Tis believed evil is where you find it,
And it can strike from anywhere.
Well, take it from me, that true it be;
And, boys, I've seen my share.

From a thousand ports on the seven seas,
I've known hell of every kind
And terror that can chill your blood
And burrow deep in your mind.

'Twas such a thing that we stumbled across,
Myself and the good ship, *Mary Dee*.
'Twas a thing from the nether realms that sailed into sight,
Riding the swells on a stormy sea.

A green and clinging mold covered her,
And her sails hung in tatters about her mast.
But for that, she must have been a handsome brig
In days long gone past.

But now, something eerie surrounded her,
A foreboding, if you will.
As we put out a crew to board her,
On the nape of my neck I felt a tingle, a chill.

The wind was causing the rigging to creak
As we reached her. But not another sound did we hear.
Sailors of that time being a superstitious lot
All hung back in fear.

Well, boys, you all know me,
And I'm bound to say that I know you, too.
I hope what I'm gonna tell you, bein' it's me tellin',
You'll take as gospel true.

For the horrors that lay in store for us as we
Boarded her are still with me to this day.
Had I known what lay in store for us
We'd have let the Hell Ship sail away.

▶

Mountain Yarns and Prairie Tales

Not a living thing did we find,
And of her crew, except for the officers, not a trace.
We found the Captain dead in his quarters,
A look of stark terror upon his face.

In the galley we found everything in order,
Everything all ready for the meal.
At the helm what was left of the First Mate,
His hands lashed to the wheel.

At the open door to her hold,
A place as black as sin,
We found the ship's dog as dead as the Captain,
His lips curled back in a horrible grin.

The life boats were still in their places.
No attempt at a launch that I could see.
Matey, can you see it? For some ungodly reason,
Eighty able seamen had hurled themselves into the sea.

In the crew's quarters
We found very little out of place.
Clothes hung in their lockers,
The weapons in their case.

And, boys, weirdest of all,
You could feel something didn't want us here,
Something old and very evil,
That the end of our time of grace was drawing near.

By God, I swear you can feel it now,
Clutching your heart, threatening to cut off your breath,
Something so repulsive and fearful that even the bravest
Threw himself over the railing to face an awful death.

Well, whatever it was would have to wait 'til morning,
As evening was drawing near.
We left to go back to the *Mary Dee*,
Leaving only a small group of volunteers.

FROM THE PEN OF BIG IRV LAMPMAN

They were armed to the teeth
With heavy weapons and cutlasses issued to everyone.
If anything braced this bunch,
They would be shot to bloody pieces under the seamen's guns.

Now we finished our supper,
And then settled down for the night.
There wasn't the usual card games and talk.
We were a pretty subdued bunch all right.

Everyone of us was thinking of our shipmates
We'd left aboard the Hell Ship we had in tow.
What we'd find in the morning aboard that floating nightmare
Not one of us could know.

Then just after midnight, the sound of screams
Brought us to the rail,
Terrible heart-wrenching pleas for help,
But we could get no answer to our hail.

In the light from the ship's lanterns we could
See men running to and fro.
The screams becoming weaker, then stopping altogether,
Nothing moving in the lantern's glow.

It would have been suicide to try to launch a boat then,
With the heavy swells, to go to our companion's aid.

At dawn we struck out to board her,
Our hearts in our throats. Then as we stood again
Aboard the Hell Ship, our courage began to fade for
We were met with silence, not a trace was there of our men.
For as sure as I'm a born sinner, whatever ungodly thing walked this ship,
Lord help us, had struck again.

The worst of it was the guns,
Fully loaded but cast aside.
Fully armed men, seasoned veterans, dropped their weapons
And fled in panic over the side.

▶

That was the only answer. No blood stains,
No trace of violence of any kind.
You'd have thought at least one would have gotten off a shot.
Why no one did just boggles the mind.

I led a bunch of men down into the hold,
Searching for who knows what.
When at last we stood again on deck,
I ordered it bolted shut.

As we stood there looking
At each other in disbelief,
Suddenly a feeling of intense horror swept over us,
A feeling of terror and evil and grief.

Our hair stood up and our scalps tingled.
Our hearts threatened to burst from our chests.
A stench assaulted our nostrils of something old and putrid and
Overpowering with the stench of death.

Panic gripped us, everyone, and then from deep in the bowels of the ship
Something moved, and a groan like a thousand lost souls assailed our ears.
As panic rushed through us, our hearts were threatening to burst
As every man screamed in fear.

As one, we fled back into the boat.
Some too slow, I'm ashamed to say, were nearly left to watery graves.
Trying to get back to our own ship,
Mightily we battled the waves.

Then, finally, we were back aboard our own vessel.
I myself cut the line and the Hell Ship drifted away.
To this day it's there in my mind.
What ungodly thing is still out there for some other poor souls to find!

If we'd done our duty, we'd have burnt
That vessel of terror to the waterline.
For in this world there are things so evil,
So repulsive, so foul, as to defy death and time.

FROM THE PEN OF BIG IRV LAMPMAN

I know this, to be aboard that Hell Ship
Made my flesh crawl, giving a ragged edge to my breath.
I've known fear before, boys, and in thirty years
I've never faltered, even in the face of death.

But never before have I stood in the presence
Of such evil as I did on that ship of Hell.
What it was I can only guess, as can you,
After you've heard this tale I have to tell.

The question remains. What could cause brave men
Who have faced the maelstrom and gale
To go crazy and destroy themselves in terror,
Ignoring heavy caliber weapons and hurling themselves over the rail?

What made the hair along my arms stand up,
And what took my breath away?
Something incredibly ancient and full of hate,
Abandoned even by God himself. I don't know what else to say.

Well, my time on the sea is over now.
I'm content to sit here in my rocker and gaze out to sea.
But, boys, you know there's one thing that, when the sun goes down
And the wind is moaning around, that still bothers me:

We didn't destroy that thing. We should have pursued her
And sent her to the bottom, down to Davy Jones.
That's what haunts me when the lightning flickers out there on the swells,
And this old sailor sits here alone.

For somewhere the Hell Ship rides the waves with her terrible occupant.
For unless destroyed, evil is really never gone.
And for time eternal
The Hell Ship sails on and on.

THE SARGASSO

Now, a bunch of us guys was a-raisin' hell
In a bar called the Sea Wolf's Lair.
We were drinkin' hard and swappin' yarns,
The kind that would raise your hair.

Now, there was Harold and me and Mysterious Dave—
A wilder crew you'll seldom see.
Then the stories got around, like they always do,
To the place called the Sargasso Sea.

The Sargasso is named for a weed
That catches a ship and holds it fast.
It was the end for many a seagoing man
In the days long gone past.

For, in the days of the sailing vessels,
They didn't have the strength to break free.
So they stayed to await their lingering doom
There on the Sargasso Sea.

It's called the Sea of Lost Ships,
And, it's no doubt, lost they be,
Caught in the weed like a fly in a web,
Never to break free.

And legend has it that somewhere in there,
Past the fog and the weed and the unearthly gloom,
Long lost ships and long dead men
Sail on, on a sea of doom.

There's pirate ships and merchant vessels
And British men of war
With rotting sails and empty eye sockets,
Faces frozen in the grip of horror.

There's nothing to eat and nothing to drink,
Though there's water everywhere.
Just mention the place and you'll see brave men
Cringe in the clutch of fear.

FROM THE PEN OF BIG IRV LAMPMAN

They say the kraken's there, lurking
To clutch and pull you down.
The fog moves in and blankets the place.
Ships disappear without a sound.

Yeah, a bunch of us boys were a-raisin' hell.
Such a crew you'll seldom see.
And we all thanked God we've never been
Caught becalmed on the Sargasso Sea.

Chapter 4

Railroad Stories and Truckers

A no more exciting time in the history of the world was the beginning of the age of steam, the railroads. Smoke belching behemoths crossing the country and along with them the railroad men and their stories. The highways that wander across our land are home to a very different breed of man. It takes a very skilled man to tame and guard the eighteen-wheel behemoths that move the country and to make the interstate home.

WHEN THE REAPER COMES

'Twas a miserable night out there in the yard,
And I was trying to get out of the cold.
But most of the boxcars were locked up tight,
As they were in that particular place, and these cold bones were a-gettin' old.

One thing, I'd found a lantern
That somebody had left a-lyin' around;,
And, ah, here was a warehouse door left ajar.
I listened, then slipped in without a sound.

I was just settlin' down for the night,
When over in the corner I heard sort of a moan.
I switched on the light, but I wished I hadn't.
Then I heard another groan.

My hair stood up like it had a life of its own,
And a chill seemed to cause my blood to freeze.
The breath stuck tight in my lungs,
And a spasm of fear weakened my knees.

For there, on the floor, lay an old hobo.
His life was slipping away.
He gasped for each breath like it would be his last,
His skin a sickly grey.
And over him hovered a huge cowled figure
Who watched his every breath.
By the scythe he carried there could be no doubt who he was.
I was standing in the presence of Death.

He whirled toward me when I switched on the light.
I'd caught him at his ghastly work.
He hovered like some obscene, ungainly bird
Over the man in the dirt.

Then I saw his face,
And it wrenched from me a scream.
A death's head was most appropriate,
Giving life to this bad dream.

FROM THE PEN OF BIG IRV LAMPMAN

Somewhere off in the distance came the sound of a whistle.
They sound so lonesome, far off that way.
And the old hobo heard, for he tried to raise
Himself from the dirt where he lay.

The reaper seemed to be running out of patience
As the hobo's last struggles went on.
He paced up and down like a thing in a cage
And checked his watch for the approaching dawn.

Daybreak was near,
And the old fella lingered still.
I guess a soul caught between this world
And the next will do as it will.

The sufferer's breath became slower,
Then at last it ceased.
The old hobo now rode on that last train to Heaven.
His soul was at peace.

Just like that, the Reaper was gone.
His work there was done.
Then I noticed it was daylight,
And I walked into the morning sun.

I know I'll never forget what I saw that night,
And I've still got the hobo's watch.
I figured he wouldn't need it anymore.
His boots were a little tight,
But they fit, so a winter's walk ain't as cold as it was before.

The little bit of change he had in his pocket
Bought a couple of jugs of wine.
A couple of other fellas drank his health,
As I hope they'll do when it comes my time.

We left him in the shed where he died
And grabbed the next southbound train.
Heck, after the Reaper comes, wherever you are,
I reckon to you it's all the same.

THE STORY OF THE STRANGEST LOVE

It was cold in the yard that night,
With icy fingers of freezing rain.
The lightning flickering through the window of our empty caboose,
The rain beating against the pane.

We had a fire in the grates of our depot stove
To try to ward off the chill.
The coffee was weak from overused grounds,
But at least we'd had our fill.

Some of the boys were playin' cards
To pass away the night.
Their faces etched in stony concentration
In the fire's garish light.

Far off in the distance, as the night wore on,
Came the whistle of a passing freight,
Crying and moaning into the wind
As if lamenting its wandering fate.

Now, God knows where he got it, but one of the 'bos
Had a couple of jugs of pop skull mad dog wine.
It's the stuff that alters your perspective,
That'll steal away your mind.
Like that poor little fella, Hobo Jim, went crazy and died of a heart attack,
Tryin' to build steam in the busted boiler of old No. 9.

We found him dead at the throttle,
Running some long-forgotten race,
Blowing a whistle silent for fifteen years,
But there was a smile on his face.

We buried him there beside the tracks.
I guess we were the only ones who gave a damn.
Listening for passing trains and a yard to haunt—
What better for a ramblin' man?

FROM THE PEN OF BIG IRV LAMPMAN

And, speaking of haunts, there's stories of ghosts
Who ride the rails,
Long-dead phantoms riding long-gone trains,
Kept alive in hobo tales.

There's a brakeman's lantern that follows the tracks
Where long ago a brakeman died.
Then there's the story of a passenger train that left a trestle,
Plunging into the river with the passengers still inside.

Over and over the tragedy's played out,
Over and over again,
A wandering mystery etched in the annals of time,
Alien to the world of men.

You know, there's a lot to be said for a depot stove
And your brothers of the road, gathered 'round
With the cold fingers of rain a-drummin' the roof
And the wind a-whistlin' around.

The yard's a mighty lonesome place
In the lightning's flickering light.
It's a sad, sad place for a man alone,
There in the yard at night.

So gather 'round, boys, and pass the jug.
It'll help to ward off the chill.
As long as there's trains, there'll be 'bos to ride 'em,
And I'm sure they always will.

I've been from coast to coast a hundred times or more,
And yet I'm waitin' here beside the tracks ready to go again.
Though I've promised myself to settle down,
I just can't resist the sound of a lonesome whistle cryin' in the wind.

I never figured myself a stupid person,
And I hope I'm not insane.
But I guess the strangest love there is
Is a hobo's for a train.

WRECK OF THE TWELVE 51

On a cold winter's night in the mountains,
The coldest in many a night,
The wind was howlin' through the canyons,
And the moon and stars were shinin' bright.

Then through the night came a whistle.
'Twas a freight train on the midnight run.
Oh, what a terrible fate was in store
For the crew of the Twelve 51.

High above them on the mountain
An avalanche had begun to grow.
And there was no one to shout a warnin',
"Look out for ice and snow!"

The wreck was over in a moment,
And they had made their last run.
Entombed in the ice forever
Was the crew of the Twelve 51.

Poor old train,
You're gonna live again
Whenever men speak of railroads,
And whenever they think of brave men.

But they say that sometimes in the mountains
On a clear and frosty winter's night,
You can see a train go rumblin' by,
All cold and ghostly white.

There's no fire under her boiler,
And she's gone with the morning sun.
For she is only a phantom, you see,
Lost in time on a never-ending run.

FROM THE PEN OF BIG IRV LAMPMAN

Spectral faces gaze sadly from the windows.
Oh, what a terrible sight!
You'll feel a chill pass over you
As she rumbles on by through the night.

So, railroaders, be careful
'Till your work on this Earth is done
Or you might spend eternity
Like the crew of the Twelve 51.

THE WHISTLE IN THE NIGHT

Now a couple of the boys and I had holed up
Out of the wind hopin' to catch a passin' freight
'Cause the weather had turned cold as a witch's heart,
Making our bones rattle and shake.

We had a fire goin', but it didn't help much,
Not at fifty below.
Me, I was heading down to the southern lands,
Down where the cotton grows,

Maybe in the land of the bayous
Or maybe in Tennessee.
Anywhere a man could sleep out under the stars
Would just be jake with me.

There weren't many of us left now,
Not of the old timers I'd known in my day.
Just like the mighty steamers we rode
A lot of my friends had just faded away.

Diesel engines had replaced the steamers, and, in turn, were being replaced
By the eighteen-wheel behemoths rolling down the interstates.
But I hoped to have at least a few good years left.
For a man pushing sixty-five, I was in pretty good shape.

Now, you've asked me if I've had any real strange experiences
During my life on the go.
Well, yes, this night I started to tell you about. I was there and
This is the way it happened. What I saw exactly, I just don't know.

Anyway, the rest of the boys were asleep, and I'd just added to the fire
When a whistle came floatin' on the wind.
My hair just stood straight up, for it was a sound I hadn't heard for thirty years.
But, by God, there it was again.

I ran outside to look in the direction it was coming from.
And, damned if my scalp didn't prickle again.
For something was moving out there, gliding across the marsh,
That just should not have been.

FROM THE PEN OF BIG IRV LAMPMAN

Out there where no track existed
I could see a headlight moving over the ground.
And then came that whistle again,
A long, low mournful sound.

I could see the glowing cinders
And the smoke billowing from her stack.
I could see the glow of the firebox
And hear the wheels clickin' on the track.

Only a snowmobile trail followed the old trackbed,
Where the rails used to go,
And cattle graze peacefully now,
And grass and dandelions grow.

As she glided on past me
A great sadness gripped my heart.
I knew she, like myself, was but a lost wanderer
In a world of which we'd been a part.

She gave one final whistle,
Then glided out of sight.
I stood there feeling lost and alone
On that cold winter's night.

Well, boys, that's my story,
And I'll swear it's true.
But I never believed in ghosts before.
I wonder, boys, do you?

What if I'd been close enough to catch her
And climb aboard for one final ride?
I wonder if, just maybe, I'd have found
Some of my old friends inside.

If you happen to be up there in that part of the country
On a cold winter's night,
If you stop and listen you might hear that whistle,
Crying mournfully through the night.

THE SURPRISE

I guess you could say ours was a family of truckers.
My dad and all three of my brothers made their livin' out there on the road.
And I always thought some of the sweetest music in the world
Was the singin' of eighteen wheels and the barkin' of twin stack diesel
    movin' a heavy load.

And for the first five years after I left high school,
I worked in a warehouse loadin' trucks.
And I'd watch those big trucks come rollin' in.
And once we had them loaded, I'd watch them roll out again.

And I always figured to go truckin'.
But I married the prom queen; and, after a couple of years,
There was a baby and then another.
And I never did get my chance to hit the road.
And I would get the itch every so often
And wonder what life was like out there on the road.

And sometimes I'd wake up and listen to a big rig
Out there on the Interstate.
And, you know, I remember my wife getting up
To sit beside me no matter how late.

Well, a few birthdays ago, I was headed home after work,
And I was feelin' kinda down 'cause our little girl had just got married
    and left home.
'Course I knew it was only natural that
Someday she'd want a home of her own.

And when I turned the corner above our house,
I couldn't believe my eyes
'Cause the prettiest new tractor I'd ever seen was parked in our drive.
All the kids and my wife were there yelling, "Surprise! Surprise!"

FROM THE PEN OF BIG IRV LAMPMAN

After they quieted down, my wife said, "Honey, I knew you hated being
  tied down
At that job all the years the kids were home.
And I've dreaded them growing' up and leavin'
And spendin' so much time alone.

"So I saved the money for a down payment through the years. And, well,
  she's ours.
And, well, what do you say? Shall we hit the road?
Here's the keys and our first contract
Waitin' for our first big, big load."

Well, it's been a grand ten years,
And our home is eighteen wheels and the Interstate
And the freedom of the open road.
Thanks to her I made the break.

And that little prom queen I married,
Well, she warms my sleeper and keeps my books.
What more could a man ask for? A pretty little woman, the road stretchin'
  out ahead
And life between these doors.

THE ROAD IS MY HOME

I met him in a truckstop in Illinois,
And, boys, he looked like he was older than the hills.
His hair was grey and the lines runnin'
Down his face looked like they'd been carved
In stone, as age lines often will.

But I noticed his eyes were clear and steady,
And laugh lines around the corners told me that
Here was a fella it would be fun to know
'Cause he'd been a truck driver for more years
Than I'd even thought of and probably had a
Million stories about life on the go.

We got to talking shop, and I asked him where
Home was. And with a slight smile, kinda sad like,
He said, "My wife is gone now, and the kids
Got their own lives, so I never get back to
The home place anymore.

"Now, that old truck has been home to me
For over twenty years or more. And she keeps
Me warm in the winter and cool in the summer, too.
She's getting old, just like me, but she's
Got a CD player that keeps crankin' out
Those country tunes, and I've got company
On the CB and a TV in the sleeper that's dang near brand new.

"Now, her voice comin' out of those stacks,
Is one of the prettiest sounds you'll ever hear.
And old bird dog on the dash lets me know
If there's a 'smokey' somewhere near.
And, you know, I've seen more country in the
Last thirty years than most men ever do.
I've been all up and down the west coast
And seen the east coast, too.
I've been over the Great Divide a hundred
Times and through the Smokies more times than that.

FROM THE PEN OF BIG IRV LAMPMAN

And I've earned every grey hair
That keeps a-hidin' up under my hat.
You ask me if I ever get lonesome?
Well, maybe, once in a while; but, then I'll pop
In a country tape, and the old truck keeps rollin' along.
First thing you know, I'm happy as a clam,
Singing along with one of those grand old Nashville songs.

"Now, there's a little waitress, prettiest little gal
You ever seen, works in a truckstop down near Texarkan,
And she thinks the sun rises and sets in a big
Ol' diesel, ridin' with a truck-drivin' man.
You know, I've been just sittin' here thinkin'.
I bet I couldn't count the nights I went
To sleep in my sleeper with Old Red Sovine
Or Dave Dudley on the radio.
And what I'd a done without old WSM
On a Saturday night, son, I just don't know.
Course I know my time's comin'; but
I hope, somewhere up amongst those clouds,
God's got an Interstate.

"And if He does, why, somehow, I'm a gonna
Get that old truck up there past those
Pearly Gates. No matter what it takes!
Yes, sir! You ask me where's home?
Right out there waitin' in the parking lot.
That's home for me!
And, God willing, for this old gear jammer,
That's where it will always be."

Chapter 5

Sentimental Poems and Stories

These are a few poems or stories that to me touch my heart. Each one has a story to tell and maybe a lesson to be learned.

HALLOWEEN: WHAT I WOULDN'T GIVE TO BE A KID AGAIN

They snigger and snagger. They're old and haggard,
But they've all got brand-new brooms.
They're a frightful sight on this
Halloween night
As they sail 'cross the face of the moon.

They swirl and twirl around in circles,
And they snackle and cackle in glee.
When they come down
They bound around
On their crickety, rickety knees.

The scarecrow takes one look then,
Takes off like a shot—this is no place for him.
It must have seemed awful funny
To the jack-o-lantern judgin'
By his snaggletooth grin.

Something in white moves out on the lawn.
It dances in the pale moonlight.
It makes your hair stand up against your hat,
But bein' scared is the fun of it
Out here on Halloween night.

God, what I wouldn't give to be a kid again,
Able to be scared by a sheet on a line.
But I've grown too old for Halloween.
I've been caught by Old Man Time.

And witches and spooks—well, I don't believe
In them anymore.
And I don't go to parties
Or go trick or treatin' at night
Like so many years before.

FROM THE PEN OF BIG IRV LAMPMAN

And the comfort of a roaring fire
And the companionship of kith and kin—
That's the most important now.
But, just once, God,
What I wouldn't give just to be a kid again.

And, you know, the Creator must have a sense of humor
'Cause just when you're old enough to enjoy youth,
It's already gone.
And you can't believe it when you realize what you had
That you should have been enjoying all along.

But that's the way of things,
The old must make way for the new.
But those great days of youth—
Dang it—
They're way too few.

THE LOVING TREE

Just a nice old couple
Loved by everyone,
Who would always invite you in for cider or coffee spiced with conversation
After the day's work was done.

Silas played the fiddle
And Molly always had a song to sing.
Dad played the guitar and, between the three,
They'd make the rafters ring.

Silas was always there with some friendly advice,
A pat on the back, and whenever you needed a loan.
Always there to toil beside you when work needed doing,
And you were weary clear down to the bone.

You've never seen two people more in love,
Though they had to be sixty years or more.
They'd hold hands as they walked together,
As they must have done when they were young so many years before.

Sometimes in the spring you'd see Silas up on the hillside,
Picking flowers just for Molly, you see.
He'd say, "Why, I'd be glad to pick her a whole hillside,
She's such a joy to me."

At Christmas time, Molly baked
Coffee cakes for everyone.
And Silas, with a twinkle in his eye, would pass out toys
He'd been whittling on all summer, like dolls, boats, whistles and little
    toy guns.

As the years crept on, the spring in Silas' step wasn't quite what it used to be.
Molly's hair by now was white.
But they still loved each other and everyone of us,
The warmth in their eyes shining bright with an inextinguishable light.

At last, as it must come to all of us,
The Lord took Molly away.
Just said goodnight to the man she'd loved for over seventy years
And in her sleep just passed away.

From the Pen of Big Irv Lampman

Well, Silas was never quite the same
After Molly passed away.
Just seemed to get a little older,
A little grayer every day.

He planted flowers and cut the grass
And sat by her grave for hours, tears filling his eyes.
It broke our hearts with helplessness
To see him fading right before our eyes.

At the head of the grave, Silas planted a tree.
Some kind of flowering tree, so it was told to me.
When I asked him what kind of tree he had chosen,
He just said with this gentle smile, "Why, it's my loving tree.

"It'll shade Molly in the summer,
Protect her in the winter, too.
I'm sure she'll enjoy the blossoms
Every year in the spring. She can watch then come out anew."

The years have sped by with their changing seasons
And changed a boy into a man.
His hair is now gray. He has a wife of his own,
A house and little piece of land.

Above Molly's grave
Stands a mighty flowering tree.
The lower branches hand down around the grave,
Sheltering it lovingly.

Both Molly and Silas now lie side by side,
Resting peacefully.
Together in death, as they were in life,
As they both wanted to be.

Sometimes on a summer night
You can feel a stirring begin with a soft melody.
Is it only the wind? It doesn't sound that way to me.
I choose to believe it's Silas singing to his beloved Molly, from the
    heart of the loving tree.

REGRET

The war was over.
Their boy was coming home.
The guns had fallen silent over the countless graves of untold millions.
Spring grass had grown.

They were told that he'd been wounded.
There were some anxious moments then.
But, then he'd called and said he was all right.
Not to worry, he'd just rest there with his men.

A few weeks later he had called
And asked if it was all right if he brought a buddy home.
"He's very badly wounded, mom.
I've seen no one visit him. I'm afraid he's all alone."

The mother, touched by her son's concern for his friend,
Said, "Certainly, son, bring your buddy. We'll be glad to have you home."
She sent her love and his father's,
And said if he needed anything to be sure to phone.

A couple of weeks later
The boy called again.
"Mom, there's one thing I didn't tell you.
It's about my friend.

"You see, he was disfigured in the mortar blast.
His face was almost blown away.
He has no one else.
I want to bring him home to stay."

The mother hesitated a moment, then said
Maybe it would be better if his friend came for only a little while.

It would be hard answering questions all the time,
And how would they afford to keep him,
What with the cost of things today?

FROM THE PEN OF BIG IRV LAMPMAN

After a long silence
The boy said to tell his dad he loved him.

He gave his mother his love and wished her the best,
Then hung up the phone.
The mother waited anxiously for her son,
Hoping he'd soon be home.

Then one day, about a week later, the door bell rang;
And when she opened it, there were two officers—one a chaplain—
Standing at her door. A cold chill gripping her heart,
The mother asked them in, then quickly closed the door.

"Madam, I would give anything not to tell you this.
But it's something that must be done.
We found a badly disfigured boy dead in a motel room the other day.
He'd killed himself with a borrowed gun.
And tho' his face was terribly scarred, through fingerprints
We've identified him as your son."

THE DAY I BURIED OLD BLUE

Now, it was one of those days that was hard to forget—
At least for a boy just entering the world of men;
And now that the years have gone by and I've grown up,
I hope that I'll never see the like again.
For I said goodbye that day to a dear old friend,
And, of those, I've had but few.
'Twas a sad, sad day for this old boy,
The day I buried Old Blue.

He was but a few weeks old when I fished him out the river.
Somebody had tied him in a gunny sack.
I carried him home and hid him in the barn.
There was no room in our one-room shack.
But, he was something to love and care about
In a world that was cold and grim.
As the weeks went by and he started to grow,
I knew I'd never seen the likes of him.

For his shoulders fleshed out and became massive,
His jaws could break a bone.
His feet were huge, his legs long and powerful,
His glossy black coat just shone.
As we both grew we became inseparable,
As a boy and his dog often do,
And there was no doubt about it when it came to hunting,
There was never another dog like my Old Blue.

I believe that dog could track a ghost across Plymouth Rock,
And, when the city fellers came
With their high-priced hounds,
They were in for quite a shock.
For Blue was surer and faster on the trail than any dog they'd ever seen.
They tried to buy him, but he was not for sale.
I loved that old dog and he loved me.
No, sir, a friend like that is never for sale.

He'd follow me as I went off to school.
He'd spend all day there in the woods,
And I'd sneak off and go fishin' or huntin'
With him every time that I could.

FROM THE PEN OF BIG IRV LAMPMAN

When the bell rang at the end of the day,
I'd hear Blue's joyous bark.
Yes, a boy and his dog, through thick and thin,
You just couldn't tear us apart.

At night, when the cold was a-whistlin' 'round our door,
Old Blue would be let in to sleep by the fire.
Mom didn't have the heart to make him stay outside anymore,
And he was content to lie there at my feet.
He'd probably have stayed till he turned to stone.
When bedtime came and I'd go off to bed,
Blue would stay on guard by the fire all alone.
As the years went by, he didn't seem quite as fast on the trail,
And, more than once, I had to wait for him.
But the spirit was still there; and, when I'd pick up a gun,
You'd think he was a puppy again.
For he'd race around and yelp and bark,
Though I'm sure his arthritis bothered him.

Then the day came when he wasn't there
Waitin' in his place by the door.
And he didn't come runnin' when I called.
Why? He'd never done that before.
I found him there in his doghouse,
In his favorite place gazin' out the door.
But Old Blue was dead. It broke my heart.
Old Blue would romp no more.

I placed him in a grave I'd dug at the edge of the woods,
And I cried till I scarcely could see.
I hoped with all my heart that, though his body laid here,
His spirit was runnin' free.
To leave my boyhood pal there and walk away
Was the hardest thing I ever had to do.
I'd laid to rest the dearest friend I'd ever had
The day I buried Old Blue.

AN OLD MAN GOES HOME

Men say the winter was cold that year.
The temperature hovered near forty below.
And the old man shivered and shook,
Eyeing his shrinking pile of coal.

The wind howled and whistled like a thing alive
With a wail like the banshee's moan.
The old man sighed and added to the fire,
Then sat down to his supper alone.

For a while afterwards he sat and smoked his pipe,
Lost in thoughts of more pleasant days,
And he wondered just how he'd come to this,
Old and abandoned this way.

For, once, this old house was a cheery place.
Children's laughter rang through the halls.
Now only night wing sang to him,
The fire casting shadows, weird shapes upon the walls.

Down in the pantry a family of mice
Looked at the meager fare offered there,
Looked at each other and shook their heads,
Then returned to scraps under the stairs.

A self-respecting mouse could starve to death
With no more to eat then that.
And, if any more mice left this house,
There wouldn't be enough to support the cat.

The wind swirled and twirled
Under the moonlight out on the lawn.
The old house moaned and groaned, as old houses do,
As the night hours crept on.

The chill seemed to penetrate every corner
As the frost seeped through the stones.
The old house complained like a thing alive
As the wind rattled its bones.

FROM THE PEN OF BIG IRV LAMPMAN

The old man, at last, was lost in dreams
Of the girl that still held his heart.
And he smiled in his sleep, dreaming of how happy they were,
Before death tore them apart.

He dreamed of warm fields of sunlight
And of her laughter tinkling in the wind.
And he knew he'd give all he owned
Just to hold her once again.

Then he felt a gentle touch on his shoulder.
The old man was no longer alone.
A gentle voice said, "John, she's waiting for you.
I've come to take you home."

The old house still stands there,
Weather-beaten and old,
Baked in the heat of the summer sun,
Frozen by the winter cold.

Somewhere, two lovers rejoice,
Never to be parted again,
Safe in each other's arms
Away from the troubles of men.

Bodies once beat with age
Are again young and strong.
The meadows are green, the brook clear and deep.
The meadowlark sings its song.

So ends our tale of a sad winter night,
An old man broken and alone.
For he's where he's wanted to be for
So very, very long now...home.

THE LEGEND OF OLD JAKE

Our town is a quiet, little place.
At least nothing earth-shattering happens in any case.
Kids grow up and drift away.
Some do anyway, and others put down roots and stay.
But our town's got one claim to fame;
And if you like fishin', one day here and you'll never be the same.
For there's a statue of a fish at the outskirts of town,
And there's another out at the campin' ground.
Our most famous resident lives in the lake.
Here's the story, the legend, of Old Jake.

Deep in the water, amongst the rocks and the reeds and the like,
Swims a big old fish they call a northern pike.
The white men say he's six feet long;
The red men chuckle and say the white men are wrong.
There's a nine-foot fish lives in the lake.
He's a livin' legend and they call him Old Jake.

People come every year from miles around.
They pitch their tents at the campin' ground.
They use underwater cameras and sonar to search the lake,
But they've never caught a glimpse of that cunnin' Old Jake.
The spend their money like water in the stores in town.
Their blood pressure goes up as the sun goes down.
Out there in the water swims Old Jake,
Lyin' quiet in the reeds at the bottom of the lake.
Too bad nobody told them fellas what Grandpa told me years ago.
The one time he did catch Old Jake, he let him go.

You see, it kept Grandpa young for years afterward walkin' down to the lake,
Dreamin' of the next time he'd hook Old Jake.
He'd sit on the bank and throw a line in.
Jake would give a tug, then he'd tug it again.
And after all these years, I can still see Grandpa's smile,
Watchin' his pole and laughin' all the while.
Grandpa and that fish got to be best friends.
Grandpa got to be somethin' of a legend himself
Amongst the town's old men.
The only man in history of fishin' that lake
Ever to catch Old Jake.

FROM THE PEN OF BIG IRV LAMPMAN

Did he ever hook him again? I don't know,
But if he did, you can bet he let him go.

Well, Grandpa's gone now, but Old Jake's still there,
Bigger than ever he's out there somewhere.
I'd like to sit on the bank like I used to with Grandpa if I could,
And tell him at last I understood
What he meant when he said, "It ain't the catchin' that's great,
It's the fishin' that's the most fun. Time and again tryin' to catch Old Jake."
'Course there's some say a fish don't live that long, but don't believe what
    they say.
A legend can live forever; and if you're down on the water some day,
If a fish as long as your boat takes your bait and heads across the lake,
Count your blessings, friend, you've hooked Old Jake.

REPAYMENT

I had gone down to the river near my home,
Figured to get me a little fishing,
Clear out the cobwebs in my brain
And just spend some time alone.

I'd had pretty good luck, caught a creel full of panfish,
And I was just sitting on the bank smoking my pipe relaxing when I noticed
    a sack in the river go floating by,
Something was alive in that sack 'cause I could see something moving inside,
And I heard some sort of whimpering cry.

Well, I shucked my boots and dove in to pull it to the bank.
When I looked inside, God knows what I'd thought I'd find.
But here was a litter of puppies, five in all, some jughead had thrown in
    to drown.
To this day, how anybody could do a thing like that just boggles my mind.

Well, I looked 'em over; and, except for being wet and scared to death,
They looked to be in pretty good shape.
I was mighty glad I'd been there.
A few more minutes and it would have been too late.

My wife, with a little checkin' around,
Managed to give away every one of those pups to a real good home.
We didn't take one ourselves 'cause we both worked at that time,
And we'd have had to leave the little pup home alone.

Well, as the years went by, the Lord blessed us with four healthy children.
My wife was able to quit work and raise her family the way we'd
    always planned.
I got a job as a factory worker, and, I guess, I was pretty lucky
'Cause the boss was able to give me all the overtime I could stand.

Then one night, about eleven o'clock,
One of the fellas came running in and told me the bad news.
"Your house is on fire. It's all engulfed in flames,
And they're calling for you!"

FROM THE PEN OF BIG IRV LAMPMAN

My heart went right up in my throat,
And I raced home fearing the worst.
I parked out on the street and ran up the driveway,
My heart about to burst.
Oh, but then, thank God, I saw my wife come running to meet me,
And between hugs and sobs, she told me what happened late in the night.
She'd awakened to hear a dog barking all over the house.
And then she realized the place was full of smoke, and the kids were
   screaming with fright.

Well, she'd managed to get the older kids outside and was just trying to
   get back in for the baby,
When out through the door came a big, brown dog with the baby in his
   mouth, safe and sound.
He'd walked right up and, with a wag of his tail,
Laid the baby at her feet on the ground.

Well, my wife had checked the tag on the dog's collar, and the next day
We went over to thank the owner and tell him about the heroic thing his
   dog had done,
To tell him there was no greater dog under the sun.

Come to find out, it was a house that had taken in
One of those puppies so long ago.
And what brought Dusty to our house that night
God only knows.

He said the puppy I had saved had been killed by a car
Right out there in the street where he used to run.
And what made my hair prickle at the back of my neck
Was, he said the dog that saved your four kids and your wife was
   Dusty's grandson.

Five for five, plain as day,
The debt was paid.
How it happened, I guess, will always be a mystery.
But, no question about it, repayment had been made.

THE THING IN THE PETERSON PLACE

It was an old house, older than even the oldest residents of our town.
Sadly neglected, the forest creatures claimed its rooms.
Weeds and briars claimed the grounds.
The night wind mourned sadly through its halls and stately rooms;
And, rumor had it, a lonely shade dwelt there in the gloom.
For my friends and I, it was a great place to play
And explore during the day.
For we could pretend we were strong and brave of heart.
But, like all ten-year-olds, we wanted nothing to do with the place after dark.

One Halloween night, oh, I guess I was about eleven years old if I
    remember right,
My buddy Jack and I happened to wander by.
We stood there looking at the old Peterson place.
I was just starting for home when I heard a whisper from Jack,
And I turned to see a smile on his face.
"I dare you to walk up to the porch and knock on the door."
Well, I wasn't about to let him know I was afraid of the old place,
So I put on a brave front and marched right up and knocked on that door.

About a second later, we were both flying down the street,
Going so fast the leaves fairly flew from our flying feet.
The most ungodly wheezing and coughing and roaring I'd ever heard had
    answered my knock and scared us to death.
We were at least five blocks away before we stopped to catch our breath.
I looked at Jack; and, I'm telling you, his face was sheet white.
If I looked even half as scared as him, I knew we wouldn't soon forget this
    Halloween night.
"What was it?" Jack asked, looking fearfully back down the street.
"I ain't ever heard anything like that, not ever," his face still white as a sheet.
"I don't know," I answered, "That's the worst sound I've ever heard. You
    reckon we should tell our Pas or the sheriff?" I asked.
"No, I ain't gonna. They'd just say we imagined it. Anyway, Halloween's
    almost past."

Well, I laid awake most of the night trying to figure out what kinda thing it
    could be.
I didn't know if I believed in ghosts or haints or such; but, whatever it was, it
    sure scared the heck out of me.
The next evening, right after supper, I snuck down to the old place and threw

FROM THE PEN OF BIG IRV LAMPMAN

a rock up on the porch. Not a sound.
I don't know what possessed me, but I reached down and picked up
   another rock off the ground.
This time when I threw it, right behind me came that same awful sound.
The thing wasn't in the house. It was right out there in the yard with me.

I didn't even wait to look back. I just took to my heels and got out
   of there fast.
I did get to see some huge grey shape as I flew past.
I didn't wait to get a better look. I just poured on the coal and made tracks
   outta there,
My heart threatening to burst in my chest.
I don't know if I broke any records coming down that street, but I did
   my best.

When I ran in the door, I was white as a sheet, out of breath and scared
   to death.
Mom said, "What in the world?" and Pa let his pipe fall from his mouth
   like he was seeing something he'd never seen before.
And, I guess he was, too, the way I came tearing in that door.
"Pa," I hollered, "There's some kinda monster in the old Peterson place.
Call the sheriff and come with me. Bring your gun, just in case."
"Now, Son, there's no such thing as monsters. But we'll go have a look see.
You sure look like something scared the daylights out of you."
Well, he didn't take his gun, and I was so scared I didn't know what to do.

Pa and I went to the old house; and there it was, all dark and spooky in
   the moonlight.
Well, we stood there a couple of minutes; and, the next thing we knew,
   here comes the sheriff.
I felt lots better now 'cause he had his gun, and his flashlight was
   burning bright.
We walked up on the porch, and, all of a sudden, the monster started
   in again.
Like to have blown the hat off the sheriff's head, and he about half drew
   his gun.
I guess it scared the dickens out of him.
Course, by that time, I was halfway down the block.

▶

But then I heard Pa and him laughing and calling me back.
I was so scared I was tempted to keep on running, and that's a fact.
Anyway, Pa and the sheriff were laughing. So I figured whatever it was,
   they had things under control.
I still had to be talked to going into that house, as dark as it was, like the
   inside of a lump of coal.
Pa said, "Son, meet your monster."

There it was, big and brown and looking kinda like a horse, except for a
   pair of extremely long ears,
Which it laid back about that time, and let out some of those awful
   wheezings and groans and moans
That sounded like a steam engine and a blown boiler and a laugh to me.
About that time, there were a million places I'd rather be.
I knew what Pa was gonna say before he said it. A mule.
I never thought of that. I'd never seen or heard one before, but I felt like
   all kinds of a fool.
Pa said one of the doors in back had blown open, and mister mule had
   moved right in.
The sheriff said he'd check around to see if a mule was missing,
And all I could do was stand there with a foolish grin.

Well, anyway, that was the story of the thing in the Peterson place.
I figured mister mule could probably fend for himself,
But I dropped off some hay and some sugar lumps, just in case.
The old house is gone now. A supermarket stands where it used to be.
They've got a playground right where the old yard used to be.
I see a kid on the swings with a big smile on his face.
And I remember those years from long ago and the thing in the
   Peterson place.

FROM THE PEN OF BIG IRV LAMPMAN

EVERYTHING IN ITS SEASON

Father! Lord, what that word means.
Almost your whole being, least that's the way it seems.
When you're young, all of you cries out to be free,
And your Dad tryin' to hold you down. Least that's the way it seemed to me.

So the struggle begins,
Your Dad wantin' to hold on just a little longer, but knowin' he just can't win.
Here's to every father, everywhere, that even hoped when you grew up the
    work was done.
Yes, here's to every Dad, everywhere, but especially to one.

Now, when I was just a young sprout, barely out of my teens,
I couldn't wait to see the world. I was tall and strong and lean.
I was so impatient I couldn't wait to be free,
But I still recall the night I left and what Daddy said to me.

"Son, it's everything in its season, all at the appointed time.
You can't plow in the winter or harvest at the plantin' time.
You've got to sow the seed, Boy, stand back and watch it grow.
Keep your eye on the weather and your back to the hoe."

"Now, winter is a time for restin'
When the land sleeps beneath the snow,
Of buyin' seed and sharpenin' tools
And pacin' to and fro.

"Wait for the winter to break in April
Seeing the geese in the sky.
Listen to the frogs in the ponds
And hearin' the newborn cry."

Now, on the hill the first sprouts are pokin' through the ground,
And throughout all creation you can hear an awesome sound.
It's the sound of the land awakenin' and reachin' for the sun.
There ain't a farmer that will rest for miles around till the spring work is done.

Now, Daddy wasn't rich. He was an honest hardworkin' man.
His hands were big and calloused from working on the land.
He loved our mom and raised five kids on his little piece of ground.
Now he sleeps in the land he loved, about a mile and a half from town.

COUSIN CHARLEY GUARDS THE CHICKENS

Growing up in the Midwest on a small farm, I was fortunate enough to know some of the craziest bunch of people you ever saw. What they wouldn't do just wasn't worth doin'. Yet, they were all as good-hearted a people as I ever knew. I'd like to share one of the things that happened, as I witnessed this one myself. First hand, you might say.

Now, one afternoon, all of us boys was over to one of our buddies' houses. He'd heard that his Cousin Charley was gonna be out from the big city to sample some country livin'. If the truth be known, Charley was one of those guys that just couldn't stay out of trouble, kinda working on a bachelor's degree in gangsterism. His dad gave him a car, some money, and told him to get lost for a while. The best place to do that was out in the country.

So about three p.m. in the afternoon, this big, black Buick came up the driveway and stopped. Out came Cousin Charley and, man, wasn't he something! Had a suit on and even had a revolver on the seat of the car. And then he began to talk. Told us all about the city and all the fights he'd been in. Now G.W. said, "Charley, seein' as how you've been in so many fights and all, and you've got a revolver and all, how about you doin' us a favor this evening?"

Well, Charley said sure he'd help. G.W. said there's somethin' been bothering the chickens at night and would Charley take his revolver and guard the chicken coop?

G.W. and his cousin had been to town and visited one of those antique shops and bought them one of those stuffed mountain lions that had been dead since God knows when. Some of the hair was falling out, one ear was gone, and part of the lip was gone so one of those fangs kinda hung out over the lower lip. After Charley went into town to get himself some liquid refreshment, as he called it, the boys took Ol' Snaggle Tooth, as we called him, and pushed him way back under the roost in the chicken house.

We all went home to do chores and then hurried back to watch the fun. When we got there, it was full dark. The boys had tied a piece of gut line to the back of Snaggle Tooth so's we could make him move a little. One of the neighbor boys got around behind the chicken coop and started scratchin' on the wall to stir up the chickens. We whispered, "He's in there, Charley." Now, Charley had been told that it was probably a weasel or fox or somethin'. So he got his flashlight and started back under the roost. About the time his light hit Ol' Snaggle Tooth, Jim gave a tug on the gut line, and Joe gave his best imitation of a mountain lion screech.

Now, we'd been needin' to clean the chicken house anyway. After Charley left there, it was a lot easier. First off, when he left, he just sucked a lot of the mess, chickens and all, right with him and considerably loosened up the rest. Thank God, my brother had the good sense to open the door or we'd a had a door to build.

Well, so much for Charley guardin' the hen house. For the rest of his visit, he was a mighty quiet boy.

ABOUT THE AUTHOR

Irvin L. Lampman was born and raised on a small farm in Wisconsin near the village of Deerfield, about thirty miles east of Madison. He grew up with a love of country music and a seemingly ingrained love of the wilderness. Somewhere deep within him was the spirit of the frontier. And while other boys made heroes out of Roy Rogers, Gene Autry, Hopalong Cassidy, and countless other celluloid cowboys, his hero was the border scout and frontier guardian, Lewis Wetzel.

As he grew older, thanks to his parents and particularly his mother, his love of reading became more pronounced, as well as his love of country music. He recorded and toured as a singer and entertainer out west, in towns like Tombstone, Dodge City, and Bodie.

As time went on, he learned that with the stroke of a pen he could transport himself from the humdrum life of trying to keep up with the Joneses to a buffalo hunt on the plains in the 1860s, to sailing ships, to haunted houses, and to a million other places.

Irv and his beloved wife, Sandra, live in Jefferson, Wisconsin. He believes that the human imagination, when under control, is one of the greatest gifts of God.

www.ingramcontent.com/pod-product-compliance
Lightning Source LLC
LaVergne TN
LVHW091551060526
838200LV00036B/795